WARD INVESTIGATION

SEAL's Pretend Girlfriend

SEAL's Pregnant Ex-Wife

SEAL's Fake Relationship

This is a work of fiction. Names, characters, places and incidents either are the product of imagination or are used fictitiously. Any resemblance to actual persons, living or dead, events or locales, is entirely coincidental.

WARD INVESTIGATION : BOOK ONE

SEAL's Pretend Girlfriend

USA TODAY BESTSELLING AUTHOR

LESLIE NORTH

BLURB

The past threatens to tear apart his new sizzling partnership…

Not wanting to turn into his absentee father, former Navy SEAL Neal Ward originally balked at joining his father's PI agency. But when the man dies under suspicious circumstances, captivating PI Lori Hart drags Neal into the investigation. His reluctance disappears when Lori's life is threatened—so he agrees to safeguard her when she suggests they fake a relationship to catch the culprit. But it won't be easy concentrating on the case when Lori herself is so irresistible.

Lori's starting to question her insistence they remain platonic. Faking a relationship is tougher than she thought. Touching each other and acting in love is driving her crazy, especially since Neal's great at switching off their "relationship" in private. Doesn't he feel anything for her?

Turns out, he does. A lot. But his resentment toward the agency for taking priority in his father's life might win out. He refuses to fall for a PI and Lori won't quit.

If only Neal would realize what a great team they'd make…in life and love.

MAILING LIST

Thank you for reading "SEAL's Pretend Girlfriend"
(Ward Investigation Book One)

Get SIX full-length novellas by USA Today best-selling author Leslie North for FREE! Over 548 pages of best-selling romance with a combined 3643 FIVE STAR REVIEWS!

Sign-up to her mailing list and get your FREE books:

www.leslienorthbooks.com/sign-up-for-free-books

CONTENTS

1

Neal Ward couldn't stop staring into the open grave.

He felt like he was standing too close to it, because even when he looked away he could still see the gaping hole in his peripheral vision. A stark reminder of everything that would remain forever unsettled.

"I'm so sorry for your loss," a woman's voice said, moving closer to him in the grayish, overcast light.

He'd heard the phrase dozens of times since he arrived at the cemetery, the go-to platitude that assumed that he actually considered burying his father a loss. His brothers were better at faking it for the people gathered to mourn Gary Ward on the cool September day, but he managed to muster up a halfhearted nod of acknowledgement for the woman standing next to him.

She sniffled. "Your father was a wonderful man."

Neal cleared his throat and tried to come up with an appropriate response to what he knew was a lie. She was anchored beside him, seemingly unaware that she was supposed to murmur a few comforting words and then move on. When he finally glanced over he realized that he recognized the teary-eyed woman.

"Lori, right? Thanks for being here."

It was Lori Hart, his father's administrative assistant at his Detroit PI business. He'd met her the year before when his dad had shown up uninvited on Neal's doorstep in Cleveland to try and convince him to come work at the agency.

If he hadn't been so pissed about the unexpected visit he might've paused to take in the auburn-haired beauty hovering in his father's shadow. Instead, his frustration had shifted to anger and he'd fought with him. Again. And his dad had walked out, just like he always did, claiming he had important work to do. If only his family had meant more than his job…

Not that any of that was Lori's fault.

"It's good to see you again," she continued, dabbing her eyes with a tissue, then turning to face him. Same pretty hazel eyes. Same cute freckles across her nose. He stopped himself. Nope. Neal was only here to bury his dad. Then he was heading back to Cleveland the first chance he got. "I'm glad you're here."

I'm not. Luckily, he bit back the words before they escaped, and caught the eye of his older brother, Lance, across the way, shaking hands and hugging the bereaved. Lance had always been better at the niceties than Neal. Beside him was their younger brother, Ryan, who looked about as miserable as Neal felt. Yeah, the Ward brothers were all dealing with some heavy shit.

Regret. Was *that* the emotion leaving him feeling so unsettled? Because it sure as hell wasn't grief for a man who felt like a stranger. But part of him wished he could go back to the week prior and change things. Change the fact that when his dad had called him, he'd let it go to voicemail. Change the fact that instead of listening to what would turn out to be his dad's last message, he'd deleted it unheard. Change a lot of the interactions between him and his dad over the past few years.

Yeah, the old man had been a shitty parent, but now that Neal was a grown man, they could have at least learned to tolerate each other like adults without lapsing into the old fights and recriminations and hurts. But no. Their relationship had stayed thorny, and then it had ended just as it had been for pretty much the last twelve years—in silence.

"We appreciate everything you did to help my father," Neal finally said, hoping that it would end the conversation and she'd move on so he could focus on anything but the hole in the ground a few feet in front of him.

"Thanks." Lori's brow furrowed more deeply. "But … there's still more I need to do."

It was an invitation for him to ask what she meant, but he wasn't taking it. No way.

Lori's eyes bored into him until he finally turned to face her. She must have picked up a few interrogation techniques from his father, because she wasn't letting him off the hook easily. She pulled her black coat across her chest and glanced around, then moved a step closer to him.

"I think your father was murdered and I could really use your help to investigate what happened," Lori whispered, her eyes daring him to say no.

Neal frowned and swallowed hard. Dammit. "*Murdered?*"

2

———

Lori blinked at him, a flash of irritation in her eyes before it was quickly covered by concern. "I'm sorry. I shouldn't have said anything here," she gestured at the headstones surrounding them, "but I thought you should know, and I wasn't sure if we'd get the chance to talk again."

His frown darkened to a scowl as he tried to connect the dots in his head. "You think someone *murdered* my dad? Because I've seen the coroner's report and it was most definitely ruled a heart attack. He might've been an asshole..." Several mourners around them shot harsh looks Neal's way and he lowered his voice. "But he wasn't bad enough for someone to kill him."

A beat passed, then two. Lance shot him a sharp look chock full of "shut-the-fuck-up-dude" and Ryan just shook his head. Finally, Lori took his arm and drew him over to a quiet spot away from the crowd, beneath a tree. "I know you and your dad had a strained relationship over the years, but he was a good man." At Neal's incredulous look, she pursed her lips. "It doesn't matter whether you agree with me or not. I'm telling you, I'm the one who found him, and there are pieces that just don't add up. But the police won't take the case."

He sighed and stared up at the slate-gray sky. "Maybe you should listen to them. They know what they're doing."

"Yeah? Well, so do I." She crossed her arms, her jaw tight. "I got my PI license a few months ago, with your dad's help. He might not have let me work the dangerous cases with him, but he helped me hone my instincts, and right now they are screaming that this is all kinds of wrong."

He shook his head at her insistence. It wasn't that he doubted her abilities, but she'd been close to his dad and grief sometimes had people seeing shadows that weren't there. The last thing he needed right now was to get tangled up in some half-baked conspiracy theory from his dad's assistant. Or to dig deeper into the feral ball of emotions that was currently clawing up his insides over the loss of his dad. Neal took a deep breath for patience and seized his best excuse.

"Well, as much as I'd like to help you, I'm afraid I'm heading home tonight, so I won't be around. Sorry." He gave her a tight smile, then started to sidle around her to head back to where his brothers were still talking to people. "Excuse me."

"No." Lori blocked his path once more. "I won't excuse you. Gary was my friend. My mentor." Her voice caught, and damn if the sound didn't stab him right in the heart. His feet froze in place, and Neal winced as the movement jarred his bad shoulder—the injury that had forced him to leave the Navy SEALs a year earlier. It had healed as well as it was going to, but it was still sensitive. The damp fall air didn't help either.

"Look, I'm sorry, Lori. I know you were close with him, but I'm not sure what it is you want me to do here."

"Come to the office with me. Now. That's what I want." She stood in front of him, all five foot and change of her, bold as any six-foot-plus team commander he'd ever seen. She had guts, he'd give her that. "Let me lay out my case for you. Hear the evidence, then decide. If you still think there's nothing there, then I'll let you go home in peace. Promise."

He wanted to say no. Wanted to get the hell out of Detroit and never come back. Wanted to put his dad and his regrets and his pain out of his head and just get the hell on with his life, but damn if he could. His own stubborn moral code wouldn't let him. The guys on his team used to call him Superman because he liked to play the hero. Too bad it had burned him in the end. He could only hope it wouldn't burn him now, too.

Neal exhaled slowly and hung his head. "Fine. I'll give you an hour. That's it. Then I'm out of here."

"An hour it is." Lori smiled and for a moment it eclipsed the bleakness around him.

"Let me tell my brothers where I'm going," he said. "I'll meet you there."

Twenty minutes later, Neal stood at the entrance to Ward Investigation. The office was located on the third floor of an unremarkable three-story building on a downtown side street, with nondescript black awnings over the windows. From the names on the glass, there was a dry cleaner on one side of the first floor and gift shop on the other. Down the block at the corner was a coffee shop. He walked inside and headed upstairs where he found Lori, waiting by the door.

"Thanks for coming," she said, letting them inside and flipping on the lights. It was nice, if a bit small. There was enough room for two large desks, plus some storage in the back for filing cabinets and a small table. No nonsense, like the man who owned the place. Or, *used* to own it. She walked over to the neater of the two desks and sat down, gesturing toward the chair across from her. "Have a seat."

Neal found himself unable to stop looking over at his dad's desk. "Is that where it happened?"

She nodded, her eyes fixed on the spot like she was haunted by what she'd seen. "When I found him he was slumped over the desk. At first I thought he was just sleeping. He'd pulled a couple of all-nighters recently and hadn't been taking care of himself. But then when I touched his arm to try to wake him, I knew he was gone." Her breath hitched and she took a moment before continuing. "Anyway." She fussed with some papers on her desk, frowning down at them. "I noticed right off that something was not right with the scene."

"What did you see?"

"Well, first off, it looked like he was drinking a coffee from that shop down the street—which didn't make any sense. He hated their coffee. And his wedding ring was under the desk, on the floor. He never took that off."

"So you're wondering why he would drink coffee from a place he hated," Neal said, allowing her to work through her evidence even though he knew it was fruitless. "Any ideas?"

"Well, my guess is he probably didn't want to be rude to whoever he was talking to who bought the coffee for him. Gary was like that. He'd choke it down just to be polite."

"Hmm." Neal had never known his dad to be particularly polite, especially about things he didn't like. He also could have mentioned that his dad took his ring off during his brief second marriage—replacing it with a new ring—but refrained.

Neal's mom had died when he was two so he didn't have any memories of her, but it was clear to anyone with eyes that his dad had never really moved on after her death from cancer. When his half-hearted attempt at a second marriage went down in flames, he put his first wedding ring back on, the day after Neal's stepmom walked out.

Not that taking off the ring was exactly hard evidence of murder. Maybe Gary had been cleaning the ring, or had taken it off to scratch an itch. Whatever. Didn't change his mind. "Hate to say it, but I'm just not convinced. Is there anything else?"

Lori hesitated a moment, then lowered her gaze. "No."

"Right." Neal stood and straightened his suit coat, then started for the door. "Then I'll be on my way. It was nice seeing you again."

"Wait," she said, standing too fast and knocking some papers on the floor. "Shit."

Feeling like even more of an ass than he already did, Neal went back to help her pick them up. But when he knelt next to her, he noticed that she was shaking, staring at a note in her hands.

"What is it? What's wrong?" he asked, his inner protector roaring to life.

Lori handed him the note, eyes wide with fear. "I don't know why I didn't see this earlier. I guess I was just too intent on convincing you to help me. It was right there on my desk…"

Her voice trailed off as he stared down at the paper clutched in her hand. The scrawl on it was messy, angry.

Stop investigating Gary's death. Or the same thing will happen to you, bitch.

A muscle ticking in his cheek, Neal straightened, helping Lori up with him. "You should hand this over to the police. Let them take it from here."

After a moment, she shook her head, frowning. "But what if whoever sent that note finds out I told them? If they're mad about *me* investigating, how much angrier will they be if the police show up and start digging? Besides, these days, the police basically hang up as soon as they hear my voice on the phone. I doubt I could find anyone to take me seriously."

"Even with the note?" Neal argued. "Isn't that proof that something's really going on here?"

"They'll probably claim I wrote it myself."

For a short, shameful second, he had actually wondered the same thing himself, thinking it might have been a ploy to pressure him into helping her. But almost immediately, he'd dismissed the thought. Her face had gone deathly pale when she'd read the threat, and while he didn't know her that well, he doubted she was that good an actress. And he'd seen the same fear in the eyes of many a soldier on the battlefield when their lives were in danger. No, she hadn't written the note. But that didn't mean the police would believe her.

She perched on the edge of her desk, her expression shifting from worried to resolute. "I think the best way out of this is through. Like your dad always said. I'll keep investigating his death, but I'll keep it secret—that way, I'll be safe." She paused. "As long as you'll stay and help."

He wanted to argue with her. *Stay?*

Neal glanced around the small room again. He hated to admit it, but the note changed everything from grief-induced speculation to something real. The only options were to let it go…or to keep investigating, secretly. He thought again about his father's death, his brain churning through the facts. His dad had been healthy. No history of heart problems, either. For him to drop dead all of a sudden seemed odd. Not that it didn't happen, but it was rare without some underlying condition. If his father really had been murdered, then a killer was walking around free—and Lori was right in his crosshairs.

Well, shit. Looked like his hero's heart had just landed him right in the thick of it again.

Neal gave her a stern look across the desk. "If I stay—and it's still a big if—we'll need a cover story. Whoever wrote that note will be watching."

She bit her lip. "Yeah, you're right."

They both went silent and Neal racked up all the ways that what he was considering doing felt wrong.

"What if we pretend to be… dating?" She offered in a shy voice. "It would explain why you'd be hanging around, spending time with me. We could say we met last year, which is true, and kept in touch. Then when you came home, we continued where we left off, and now you're sticking around so we can see where things go."

Neal scrubbed a hand over his face. He didn't like it. Not at all. But he didn't have any better ideas. "I want it clear between us that this is just pretend. One-hundred-percent platonic."

"Absolutely." She gave a curt nod. "You know, for years, my go-to line whenever nosy neighbors or relatives or skeevy guys in bars asked if I was seeing someone was to tell them that I was in a long-distance relationship, then change the subject. So, from my end, this fits in fine." She frowned. "Of course, I'll have to tell my sister the truth, since she won't buy my falling in insta-love, but I think everyone else will believe it."

If only Neal had it so easy. He could just imagine what his brothers were going to say when he told them. And unfortunately, that would have to happen sooner rather than later, because he had to get his stuff from their dad's place. If he was staying in Detroit for more than the two nights he'd planned, he sure as hell wasn't staying there. Too many bad memories. Too much pain.

"Fine." He stood again. "I'll find a hotel room. Where do you live? I want to be close by in case of trouble."

Lori opened her mouth, then closed it. "Why don't you stay with me?" He started to protest, but she held up a hand. "I have a three-bedroom house and it's just me right now, so it's fine. We'll be roomies. Nothing more. Besides, in case of trouble, you'll be right there."

Dammit. She was right again. It was a pattern he wasn't enjoying. "Okay. I still need to go to my dad's to get my stuff."

"Perfect." She hopped off the desk, purse in hand, and walked with him to the door. "I'll come with you."

3

―――――

Lori sat in the passenger seat of Neal's SUV, still feeling a bit shaken as she thought about that note. Sure, she hadn't locked the place up as tight as she normally would because she'd been hurrying to get to Gary's funeral and swamped with grief, but still, the fact that someone had been in there was unsettling. Nothing felt quite safe now, not even her car, which Neal had insisted they leave behind at the office, saying he needed a chance to sweep it for potential threats before it was safe for her to drive. He said he thought a bomb was unlikely, but was still a possibility—along with listening devices.

She shook her head and tried to focus on something else. Like the fact that Neal had agreed to help her investigate. She obviously could use his skills and expertise from the military, but she'd been fully prepared for him to say no. Working so closely with Gary the past few years had given her a good insight into their relationship—rocky at best and downright hostile at worst. And from the perma-scowl on his face all day today, it was clear he wasn't thrilled to be here.

It had been a hard day for both of them, for lots of different reasons.

As they headed through downtown Detroit, past the glowing lights of the Fox Theater and out toward the suburbs, she couldn't help sneaking glances at Neal from the corner of her eye. Gary had kept pictures of his sons on his desk at work, and many an afternoon, when it was slow, Lori found herself staring at them, imagining what the men in the pictures were like. Neal's had been of him in his dress whites, looking pristine and perfect. Secretly, she'd always had a tiny crush on him, not that she'd ever tell him that. Nope. This arrangement they had was strictly professional.

With a sigh, she rolled her stiff neck and glanced over at him again as they turned the corner onto the street where Gary lived. Still so weird to think he was gone. "This must be so hard on you and your brothers, dealing with all this so unexpectedly."

"Hmm," Neal grunted, not looking at her. "Wasn't what I expected to be doing this week, that's for sure."

"Is there a lot to do to settle his estate?" she asked.

"I don't know," Neal bit out as he turned into the driveway of his dad's two-story colonial and parked. The headlights switched off automatically, leaving them sitting in sudden dark silence. He tapped his fingers on the steering wheel, as if burning off excess energy. "I'm not really involved in all that. Left it up to Lance and Ryan since they were closer to Dad than I was." He ducked his head slightly to peer out at the glowing front windows of the house. "We should get in there so I can get my stuff. Don't want to be too long."

He got out of the car, leaving her to trail after him. She didn't hold his rudeness against him, knowing funerals made people act weird.

Lori walked up onto the porch just as Neal opened the door. Inside, she saw Lance, his suit jacket gone and his dress shirt sleeves rolled up, sitting on the sofa with a beer in one hand and his feet on the coffee table. Ryan was chilling in the recliner across from him, sans drink, his shoes off and his stockinged feet elevated on the footrest. They both looked about as exhausted as Lori felt.

"Hey, bro," Lance said. "What's—" His voice halted as Lori stepped inside behind Neal and closed the door. He frowned and straightened, hiking the bottle in her direction. "—going on? Miss Hart."

"Lance," she said, giving him a weary smile. "Please call me Lori."

"Lori it is then," he said, nodding politely. Lance was always polite, if maybe a little formal. Lori had always gotten the impression that he didn't let his guard down easily. He was a Navy SEAL, too, though Gary had mentioned that Lance had recently been promoted out of active duty and into a desk job at the Pentagon—and that he was none too happy about it. "What brings you here tonight?"

"Oh, Neal needed to pick up his stuff, and he and I wanted to spend some more time together, so…" she started. She looked to Neal for him to pick up the story, figuring he'd know what to say to convince his brothers, but he just stood there awkwardly silent.

"Why do you need your stuff? Are you heading back to Cleveland right now?" Ryan asked, frowning. "I thought you were sticking around at least for the night."

"I'm not leaving town," Neal grumbled as he walked through the room and down the short hall to one of the guest bedrooms. "But I'm not staying here. I'll be at Lori's."

Ryan and Lance's gazes both snapped back to her. Heat prickled her cheeks, and she opened her mouth to explain, but Neal beat her to it.

He came out of his room with a black duffle bag in one hand and plopped it down on the hardwood floor near the door. "Look, it's not a big deal, okay? She and I have been dating a while and we want to spend some extra time together before I leave."

"Uh, wait a minute, dude." Ryan was up and across the room now, stopping a few feet away from them and looking skeptical as hell. "You're dating? Since when? And why didn't you tell us?"

"I don't buy it." Lance frowned. "When the hell did you two meet?"

"Last year, when Dad and Lori came to Cleveland."

"And you kept this to yourself until tonight why?" Lance countered. "Sorry. Sounds fishy to me."

Neal scowled, avoiding eye contact even as his brothers closed in on him. "I really don't care how it sounds to you, bro, because it's none of your business anyway."

"Who flipped your dick switch tonight, dude?" Ryan chimed in, the tension level in the air rising into the red zone.

Yeah, this was getting uncomfortable as hell. Lori wasn't a great liar, but Neal was even worse. If they weren't careful, he'd blow this whole thing before it even started. She inched toward the open kitchen off to the side of the room in hopes of giving the brothers a moment to work it out.

"I'm, uh, just going to get some water," she mumbled, though she doubted anyone was listening. She grabbed a glass from the cabinet near the sink and filled it with water, doing her best not to eavesdrop on the conversation from the living room and failing miserably.

Neal kept trying to sell the line about them hitting it off in Cleveland and keeping in touch, but when that wasn't enough to convince Ryan and Lance, he pivoted. "Okay, fine. There's a little more to it," Neal said. "She thinks she might've picked up a stalker working one of her cases. She's scared, so I'm going to stay with her, keep an eye out for any trouble and see if I can help her get to the bottom of it. It's not like I'm in a huge rush to get back to Cleveland. I'm getting a decent amount of freelance security work, but it's not like the town's going to fall apart without me if I'm gone for a week or so. I'll be more useful here. And yeah," he added, "we'll be seeing where our relationship goes while I'm here too, okay? God, you guys are way nosier than I remember."

And maybe Neal wasn't such a bad liar after all.

A beat or two ticked by. Then Lance finally said, "Now that I buy."

"Yeah, dude. Way to step up," Ryan added.

Lori finished her water and joined Neal by the door again in time to say her goodbyes. As they headed back outside, she couldn't help whispering, "Nice cover."

"Thanks," Neal said, hitting the button on his key fob to open the back tailgate, the headlights flashing twice. "I had to think on my feet a tad there."

"But why not just tell them the truth?" she asked. "Obviously, we need to keep up the cover story with most people, but it's different with family. I'm going to be telling my sister the truth—I wouldn't mind if you told your brothers. They're both special operatives, so it's not like they don't know how to keep a secret."

"Not until we know for sure what happened," Neal replied firmly. "They were closer to Dad, like I said. I don't want them to know we think he might've been murdered until we have more answers."

They didn't say anything more on the short drive over to Lori's place, which was fine with her. Her head was still spinning from everything. Hopefully, a good night's sleep would clear her mind. She gave him directions as they drove and ten minutes later, they pulled up outside her ranch-style bungalow.

"Stay here," Neal said, sliding out from behind the wheel, then digging in his duffle bag to pull out a gun. "Give me your keys. I want to sweep the place before you go inside."

She passed him the keys, then waited in the car, feeling torn. On the one hand, it felt like overkill. After just one threatening note, it was highly unlikely her life was suddenly going to become a Michael Bay movie. On the other hand, it was nice to know he was taking the threat seriously and that he was committed to keeping her safe. She was used to looking out for herself—it was nice to have someone else on the job for a change.

The sound of the car door opening again jarred her from her thoughts. Her house was lit up like a Christmas tree now and Neal was returning his gun to his duffle bag.

"All clear," he said, then waited on the sidewalk for her as she got out.

Lori followed him up the path to the front door, doing her best not to notice how his muscled arm brushed hers as they walked or the fact that he looked pretty damned hot when he went into stern-protector-SEAL mode. They went inside and she locked the door behind them, then released the breath she'd been holding.

It felt good to let go of a little tension. She'd been around enough PI investigations to know that a case like Gary's wouldn't be over fast, and if she spent the whole time feeling terrified, she'd burn out and make mistakes. When she found a moment of respite, she needed to make the most of it.

She toed off her pumps, sighing in relief as her sore feet hit the cool hardwood, then headed for the kitchen. "How about a beer?"

While she was at the fridge, she pulled out a frozen pizza and put it in the oven to bake. She hadn't eaten since breakfast and her blood sugar was getting low, which made her cranky.

"No thanks," Neal said, frowning. "I'd like to unpack and get some rest. Oh, and we're getting you a security system for this place first thing in the morning."

"Right." She flashed him a tired smile, then led him down the hall to her guest room, flipping on the lights to reveal a bare-bones space with a full-sized bed and dresser and not much else. The walls were a light pink and there was a stuffed bunny on the bed. She didn't have a lot of people stay over these days, other than her niece, Hope, and pink was her favorite color. Lori walked over and picked up Mr. Fluffy, tucking him out of the way in the closet. "Probably not your preferred color scheme, but it's clean and comfortable and should work for the short time you're here."

"It's fine. Thanks," he said, brushing past her to set his duffle bag on the floor by the bed, then starting to unpack.

"So, tell me about your life in Cleveland?" Lori said, twisting the lid off her beer bottle and taking a sip. Damn. The cool liquid hit the spot after a long, hard day. "What do you do for fun?"

"I work," Neal said, his tone flat.

"That doesn't sound like fun at all," she teased, hoping to draw him out of his shell. "Come on. We're stuck with each other for a couple days at least. And we're going to be playing at being a couple. We need to get to know each other at least a little. What are the stories that anyone who knows you well would know?" Lori leaned a shoulder against the door frame and grinned. "Bet you got up to all kinds of hijinks when you served, eh? Where were you stationed? Any cool countries?"

He gave her a few monosyllabic answers and she drank more beer, the alcohol hitting her harder than normal because of her empty stomach. Rather than stand there and talk to the wall that was Neal, she decided to check on the pizza.

By the time it was done, he'd finished unpacking and had joined her at the bar in the kitchen to eat. She passed him a plate with a slice and a napkin, then settled on the stool beside his. He finally took her up on the beer and by the time he finished it, he'd unbent enough to start talking in complete sentences. She kept trying to draw him out, and eventually, he told her about one time when his SEAL team had been stationed in Tunisia and they'd snuck onto one of the Star Wars sets to try and get pics with the stars.

"That sounds majorly cool," she said around a bite of pepperoni. "Did you get to meet George Lucas?"

"Nope." Neal grinned over the top of the beer bottle. "I saw him from about ten feet away and was going over to talk to him when security caught us."

"Oh no!" Her eyes widened. "Did you guys get in trouble?"

"Nah, they let us go when they found out we were servicemen. Did get a warning not to come back, though. Or tell anyone what we saw. Top-secret and all that."

"Wow." She finished her last bite of pizza and wiped her mouth, saying without thinking, "You've done awesome stuff. No wonder Gary was always so proud of you."

At the mention of his father, Neal shut down again, his smile disappearing behind the stoic façade. He stood and cleared his dishes and threw away his trash before heading back to his room with his beer. "Thanks for dinner. I'll see you in the morning."

Lori watched him go, wishing she could kick herself in the butt for ruining what had become a not-so-terrible evening.

4

———————

The next morning Neal was up and ready to go before the sun rose, as usual. Old habits were hard to break and even after the abrupt end of his SEAL career, he'd kept on with the whole "up at dawn" deal because it helped him be more productive with his days.

That and he needed to take his meds to keep the pain in his right shoulder under control.

He padded out to the kitchen in his stocking feet and set about trying to make a pot of coffee. Found the machine fine, but the supplies were a bit more challenging. After quietly digging through Lori's startlingly messy pantry, he located filters and a canister of coffee behind a haphazard stack of expired boxes of cereal and crackers. Once he got a pot brewing, he quickly organized her shelves, then went to put the coffee canister in the fridge, where it belonged. When he opened the door, he found the shelves in there even more of a mess than the pantry had been—which was surprising since she didn't have much of anything in there.

Neal put the coffee on a shelf in the fridge, then stared at the jumble of yogurt containers, a couple of half-used loaves of bread of different varieties, and the empty jug of milk in the door. Curious, he closed that and opened the freezer door to find all manner of frozen dinners. Not exactly healthy fare.

The coffee maker stopped humming. He poured himself a cup of liquid energy and took a seat at the island bar where they'd eaten the night before, a pad and pen in hand. If he was going to be staying here, they'd need groceries. He liked to stay in shape and a diet of nothing but processed foods didn't fit the bill. Plus, well, he felt bad about how he'd acted the night before. It wasn't Lori's fault that his father had been a shitty parent, and if her innocent comment about a man she only knew from a professional standpoint triggered him, that was Neal's problem, not hers. Maybe he could start to make amends for being such a grouch by treating her to some decent groceries.

He'd just finished making a list when he heard the sounds of the shower running in the master bath.

As part of his "play nice" campaign, he got to work making breakfast for them. There wasn't a lot of choice, but there were eggs and toast, so that was what he went with. A lot of people were surprised he knew how to cook, but Neal liked it. It helped relax him. He liked the precision of it, and he'd had a lot of practice too, growing up. With Dad never around, and his stepmom gone by the time he was eight, it had been up to Neal and his brothers to learn how to handle the chores. Cooking had been his favorite. By the time he was eleven, when eighteen-year-old Lance had graduated high school and joined the navy, Neal had taken over pretty much all of the cooking. Back then, he'd made breakfast for himself and his little brother every day, and dinner most nights too.

"Hey," Lori said, wandering into the kitchen behind him while he worked at the stove. "Whatcha doin'?"

He shrugged, using a spatula to tease the browned edges of the scrambled eggs away from the edge of the pan before plopping in his secret ingredient—American cheese slices. "Making us something to eat."

"Oh." She poured herself some coffee and gave him some side-eye. "That's nice of you."

"Figured it was the least I could do," he said, glancing over at her and doing his best not to notice how good she smelled. Her shampoo had this tropical, flowery scent that reminded him of Hawaii. Against his wishes, his gaze flicked down to the robe she was wearing, pink and soft-looking and stopping at her mid-thighs and…

Whoa, Nelly.

Neal forced his eyes back to hers, blaming the heat climbing up from beneath the collar of his black T-shirt on the stove. Yep. That was it. His voice emerged more roughly than he'd intended. "Hope you like scrambled eggs."

"Sure. What's not to like?" She smiled and made her way over to sit at the island. She sipped her coffee leaning forward slightly and closing her eyes, her flushed cheeks making him wonder what other circumstances might cause her to turn such a lovely shade of pink.

Stop it. He was here to work, not get laid. And sure, maybe it had been too long since his last intimate relationship. That didn't mean now was the time to hook up again, no matter how tempted he might be. Getting involved with his dad's old admin and friend had *huge mistake* written all over it.

Scowling, he turned back to his eggs in time to keep them from burning and busied himself by pulling two plates from the cabinet before serving up a portion of eggs on each.

"Anything I can do to help?" she asked from behind him.

"Put some toast in," he mumbled, shoving the now empty pan in the sink to soak. "I wasn't sure what kind of bread you liked so I set them all out. I'll take wheat."

"Wheat it is then."

He gathered napkins and silverware, then carried them, along with the plates, over to the island and set one batch in front of Lori before taking a seat on the stool beside hers. The toaster dinged and the bread popped up. She leaned over to grab it, her arm brushing Neal's, and he damned near swallowed his tongue. Not from the contact, though that was bad enough. But when she reached to grab the toast, her robe eased open a bit and he had to look away fast to avoid seeing a whole lot more of Lori than he had a right to. Mouth dry, he chugged more coffee and prayed for mercy.

If she noticed anything odd in his behavior, she didn't mention it. Just chatted on about the food and the case while Neal tried to get his errant libido back under control.

Times like this he missed his SEAL team more than ever. Breakfast had never been charged like this around them.

The meal passed in a blur, and afterward, Neal cleaned up the kitchen while Lori finished getting dressed. Then they were off to the office. The sun was out today, and though the weird haze of grief and anger still clouded his mood around the edges, he could appreciate that at least the weather was better. He parked the SUV and they walked the half a block up to his dad's building. Inside the small foyer stood a nondescript white guy, medium-height, thin and pale, unlocking the door to the dry cleaners. Guess those perfectly pressed, spotless clothes of his made sense, given where he worked.

"Hey, Lori," the guy said, giving her a polite smile over his shoulder.

"Hey, Curtis," she replied, stopping at the bottom of the stairs. "This is my boyfriend, Neal Ward. Neal, this is Curtis Hill. He owns the dry cleaners."

"Nice to meet you," Neal said, raising his chin toward the guy and placing his hand on Lori's lower back to keep up the façade. Not such a wise decision, in hindsight, given how good it felt to touch her. Too late now, though, so he kept his hand there anyway, ignoring the fizzing awareness prickling up his arm.

"Same." Curtis frowned and turned toward them. "Wait. Ward? Were you related to Gary?"

"He was my dad."

"Oh, jeez. I'm so sorry for your loss," Curtis said. "He was a really great guy. Such a shame he's gone now."

"Yeah." Neal's strained smile dissolved completely at that. Everyone loved his dad, apparently. Except they'd never had to be raised by him. He turned and headed upstairs, leaving Lori and Curtis to stare after him. "I need to make a call. Excuse me."

He reached the third floor, then realized Lori had the keys.

Luckily, she followed not too far behind him, giving him a look as she moved in beside him to open the door. "Okay?"

"Fine," he said, pushing into the office without any further explanation and flipping on the lights, checking the area before allowing her inside as well. "So, what's on the agenda this morning?"

"Well, if you want to start going through your dad's files on his most recent case, that would be good. I'd tried to convince your dad since I started here to go digital, but he wouldn't do it, so it's all still paper."

"And what are you going to do?"

"I'm going to keep working on our current contracts," she said, taking a seat behind her desk. "It's mainly just background checks for corporations, which I was already doing anyway, before Gary died. I contacted our current clients after Gary died to let them know the situation, and to give them the option of moving over to another firm who agreed to take on some of our load, or staying with me. One client chose to drop her investigation entirely, and most of the trickier cases decided to go with a more experienced team, but I have enough to keep me busy and to keep my paycheck coming and the lights on. It's a shame about some of those cases we lost, though."

"Why?" he asked, stepping over to his dad's area. In Neal's mind, the less risk Lori put herself in at present, the better. "I like that you're sticking with simpler stuff. That's the smart thing to do."

She snorted. "Well, safe won't find out who killed your dad." At his sharp look, she cringed. "Sorry. It's just that your dad mostly shut me out when it came to his dangerous cases. And now that he's gone, that leaves me in the dark, which is frustrating because I think that last case he was working on got him murdered. If only he'd let me tag along, or at least talked to me about it like he usually did, I might have a better idea of what we're dealing with."

Neal exhaled slowly and sat forward to start going through the stacks of files on his dad's desk. "Well, then I'd best get started, huh?"

But sitting at his father's desk, seeing the familiar knick-knacks and photographs, he couldn't help remembering how much his dad had poured into his work—and how it had caused him to miss out on everything else. And the more he remembered all those missed birthdays or basketball games or baseball games, the more pissed Neal became.

"Great guy, my ass," he mumbled under his breath as he closed one file and opened another, Curtis's words from earlier echoing in his head.

"I'm sorry?" Lori looked over at him, frowning.

"Nothing." Neal scowled down at the client sheet in front of him.

Please drop this, he silently pleaded with her. He did not want to get into this with her again right now. He still felt too raw, too vulnerable, too upside-down inside about it all.

Except no, she wasn't going to drop it, because she got up and walked over to him, a sour expression twisting her pretty face. "Look," Lori said, stopping in front of his dad's desk. "I realize that things between you and Gary were strained, and that you're still dealing with what losing him means to you, but I lost someone too. Your dad was my friend. And no matter how you felt about him, I'm not the kind of person who just sits around and lets someone talk shit about my friends. So, if you can't at least be civil when you mention him, then maybe it's best if you don't say anything at all. Understand?"

With that, she walked back to her desk and sat down, leaving Neal to stare after her, torn between affront at her dressing him down like that, and respect for her courage at confronting his bullshit.

5
____

Luckily, by the time Lori's mom dropped off her niece Hope for babysitting later that afternoon, Lori had her emotions back under control. She hadn't meant to lash out at Neal like that, knowing he was going through a lot, but damn. Hearing him disrespect Gary over and over rubbed her the wrong way. No one was perfect, Lori knew that. But Gary had been like a father to her, looking out for her, protecting her, encouraging her when no one else would, and she couldn't stand to hear his own son say such horrible things about him.

The bell above the door chimed and she looked up to see her mom and Hope walking into the office. Her mom's gaze immediately went to Neal, who was still up to his neck in paperwork behind Gary's old desk, then back to Lori, a question lurking in her eyes. Hope was more direct in her curiosity, just making a beeline straight for Neal.

"Who are you?" the little girl asked, with full five-year-old bravado, standing with her hands on her hips about two feet from Neal's chair. "Why are you sitting at Uncle Gary's desk?"

"I'm Neal. I'm Lori's boyfriend," he said, like it wasn't a bombshell detonating.

"Uh, sorry," Lori said, getting up and coming around her desk to corral her wayward niece. "Hope, come over here with Grandma and me. Neal's busy."

Hope frowned, her bottom lip quivering slightly. "I miss Uncle Gary."

"I know, baby." Lori came over and riffled through the desk drawers, doing her best to ignore Neal's stare burning a hole through her. She found the stash of hard candy Gary always kept just for Hope and pulled out a peppermint swirl, handing it to her. "Here. It's a special gift from Uncle Gary to remember him by. Whenever you see one of these candies, you'll know it's a sign that he's looking out for you from heaven."

Her chest squeezed at the little girl's expression, a mix of sadness and joy. "Thanks, Aunt Lori."

"She's your niece?" Neal asked, the chair squeaking beneath him as he sat back.

"Yes." She took a deep breath and forced a smile. Best to deal with the fallout now. "Neal, this is Hope—and my mom, Maggie. Hope, Mom, this is Neal. Like he said, he's my boyfriend."

"Excuse me?" Lori's mom gave her an incredulous stare—which was pretty much what Lori had expected. Not only had she never mentioned Neal to her mom before, which would be a big red flag on its own, but her mother would never expect Lori to get involved with a co-worker again. Not after the disaster last time had been. "Lori, I—"

Needing to put out this fire as quickly as possible, Lori took her mom by the arm and steered her to the far corner of the office for a bit of privacy. "I know how this looks, Mom, but Neal's not my co-worker, okay?"

"What is he, then?" her mom said, glancing over to Gary's old desk. "Because it certainly looks like he's working here and you just confirmed he's your boyfriend, so…"

"He's Gary's son. We met last year when Gary and I visited him in Cleveland. We hit it off and have been doing the long-distance thing for a while now. He's in town now for the funeral and to settle his dad's estate. He's just here today to get things in order with the business, that's all. Strictly temporary."

"Hmm." Her mother's expression was still skeptical as hell. "Are you sure this is a good idea? I don't want to see you get hurt again."

"I won't, Mom. I know what I'm doing, okay?" She took a deep breath. "Don't you have a hair appointment to get to?"

Her mom blinked at her, then shook her head and started back toward the door. "Yes. I'll be back later. I've got my phone if anything goes wrong. Be careful."

With one last judgmental look in Neal's direction, she left.

Cheeks hot, Lori slowly turned back to find Neal trying to concentrate on a file again, while Hope badgered him with non-stop questions about everything from where he was from to what his favourite kind of candy was.

Great. After how rocky their morning had been, this didn't bode well for a peaceful afternoon.

"Sorry," Lori said, rushing over to take Hope by the shoulders and move her toward an empty table in the corner where she set her niece up with paper and crayons to color with. Once Hope was sufficiently occupied, Lori returned to Neal's desk. "Listen, I really am sorry I forgot to warn you about this. I usually look after Hope once a week, to give Alison a chance to catch up on paperwork, since she's a teacher. Mom's happy to take Hope during the school day, but she uses the after-school hours for her errands and appointments, so…"

"It's fine." Neal said, giving her a genuine smile. "And I'm sorry too. About earlier. I'm under a lot of stress right now and might have over-reacted."

She wanted to ask him more about why he had a problem with Gary, but now wasn't the time. Lori glanced over at Hope and back to him, keeping her voice low. "I'm sorry too. I didn't think about it until now, but given the threat from yesterday, are you sure it's all right that she's here? I don't want to put Hope in any danger. Maybe I should take her back to my house."

"No. I think she's fine here," he said, stretching out those long legs of his, drawing attention to his taut, muscled torso. Not that she was looking. Nope. "I looked around the building earlier on a break and it's actually fairly secure. And we don't want whoever sent you that note to get suspicious, so you need to stick to your normal routine as much as possible."

"Okay." She opened up the drawer and pulled out more candy to stick in her pocket for later. Neal watched her, his expression unreadable. "What? You want one?" she offered.

"No." He shrugged. "I'm just surprised to see it there, that's all."

"Why?" Lori scrunched her nose. "Lots of people keep candy in their desks."

Neal sighed. "My dad never did. And he hated peppermint."

"Yeah, he bought those just for Hope. He'd talk her into trying a butterscotch sometimes so they could have them together, but peppermint is her favorite, and he liked indulging her."

Neal looked stunned. He blinked up at her a moment before pushing to his feet. "Guess my dad changed some since I knew him. Excuse me a minute."

With that, he walked over and took a seat next to Hope at the table, asking her about her drawing and even picking up paper and a crayon himself to sketch, leaving Lori to watch them both, a bit befuddled. Given how withdrawn he'd been yesterday and how quickly he'd slammed his walls down whenever she brought up his own family, she hadn't expected Neal to be good with kids, but he was.

Hope was giggling as he showed her whatever he'd scribbled on his paper, and Lori couldn't help grinning too. Then realization struck and she sobered up quickly. All this time, she'd thought that Neal didn't value family because he'd put such deliberate distance between himself and his father. But now she was getting the sense that the distance was *because* he valued family so much and Gary maybe hadn't, at least not when Neal was younger. Interesting. She filed that information away for later, then went back to work at her desk.

They ended up ordering takeout for dinner that night, despite all the groceries Neal had insisted they stop and buy on the way home. Neal had said he was too tired to cook, so they'd gotten delivery.

Now, as they sat across her dining room table, the air filled with the delicious scents of Kung Pao chicken and spicy egg rolls, Lori felt the knots of tension between her shoulder blades relax. Based on Neal's smile, he appeared to be feeling the same way. The moment seemed right to try and get him to open up to her again.

After washing down a bite of rice and chicken with her beer, she smiled over at Neal. "Did I ever tell you how I met your dad?"

He shook his head, swallowing a huge hunk of egg roll dipped in soy sauce. "No."

"It's pretty silly, actually. Makes me look like a real naïve idiot." She sat back and crossed her arms. "I was working at a marketing firm and dating a coworker—my boss, actually, though he hadn't gotten that position yet when we started going out. Gary was hired by one of the business partners to investigate my boyfriend for embezzlement."

"Was he guilty?"

"Oh yeah." Lori sighed. "But worse than that, he'd doctored the paperwork to try to make it look like I was the one responsible instead."

Neal paused with his chopsticks halfway to his mouth, a chunk of chicken tumbling back to his plate. "What?"

"Yeah." She gave a short laugh and shrugged, resting her elbows on the table as Neal did the same. "He knew my passwords, so it was pretty easy for him to fake. Luckily, your dad saw right through it and pulled together plenty of proof as to who was really responsible. Anyway, your dad thought I had the right to know, so he went out of his way to tell me what was going on. Good thing he did, too, because otherwise, I'd have been confused as hell about what happened. The company was desperately trying to cover everything up to keep from looking bad, so I couldn't get straight answers out of anyone…except Gary. When I decided I'd had enough of the lies and evasions and left my job, he hired me to be his admin. Gary helped me put my life back together again after it all fell apart. He didn't have to do that, but he did. And he had my back one hundred percent when I decided to get my investigator's license. He helped me, mentored me, walked me through every step—and most of all, he believed in me. That really meant a lot." She took a deep breath and pushed the rice around on her plate with a chopstick. "I guess that's why I'm so sensitive about hearing you criticize him."

"Wow. I had no idea."

"Why would you?" She raised one shoulder and flashed him a sad smile. "But that's why my mom was giving you the stink eye earlier. Seeing you at the desk, she thought we were working together, and she didn't like the idea of me having another workplace romance. She's very protective of me now."

Neal seemed to take that in a moment, then nodded, fiddling with the label on his beer bottle. "I get that."

Several beats passed as they ate more of their food. Finally, Lori's curiosity got the better of her and she tried again to draw him out. If she was going to ask him to understand her perspective on Gary, then she owed it to him to try to understand his point of view, too. "So, you didn't grow up in a fairy tale, huh?"

"Huh?" Neal gave her a puzzled look.

She smiled. "You seem really tight with your brothers, that's all. Which is good. But not so close with your dad. I wondered why."

At first, she didn't think he'd answer, since he didn't say anything for a long while. Lori feared she'd pushed him too far. But then he seemed to relax a bit, those broad shoulders of his sagging as he stared down at his plate. "There was this time when I was little. My dad was supposed to take me and Ryan to see a Tigers game for my birthday." He put down his fork, sat back, and shook his head. "Man, I was so excited that day. We waited and waited on the front porch for hours, sure every sound we heard was him coming to get us. But with every car that passed, my hopes faded. Lance was home—he'd just gotten back from basic training—and he took us inside and made us snacks while we watched a movie on TV." He scowled at his bottle on the table. "Later that night, after Ryan and I went to bed, I heard Lance and Dad fighting. He told Dad he had to make a choice. Either he could step up and be a good father to us kids or he could be a good detective, but not both. Dad chose to be a good detective."

The edge of pain in his voice made Lori swallow hard against the lump of sympathy in her throat. She'd always admired Gary's work ethic, but now she could see it had costs elsewhere in his life. "I'm sorry, Neal." She sighed. "I sometimes forget that people can show me one side of themselves in public and show a completely different one to the people closest to them in their lives."

"It's fine." His tone was quiet, and he looked up at her, their gazes catching, holding. "There's a reason why cops don't investigate the deaths of close friends or family members. It's incredibly hard to be objective in those cases."

Without thinking, she reached over and placed her hand atop his on the table. "How about we agree to be more patient with each other going forward? It's a start, anyway."

He smiled, and her heart did a little tumble as his fingers squeezed hers. "Agreed. It's a good start."

6

The next morning they were back at the office and Neal was back to work on the case files. The one that seemed most promising to him was the only file that *wasn't* still active—the investigation where the client had chosen to drop the matter entirely after his father's death rather than either transferring to a different agency or having Lori continue the work. As chance would have it, that particular client was Neal's former sister-in-law—Lance's ex-wife, Ruth. By ten a.m., Neal had stared at the damned case file for so long that his eyes felt crossed. And still he'd found nothing in there that would warrant killing his father.

Part of the problem was that there was barely anything in the file at all. His dad had chosen to be extra secretive about this case, keeping his descriptions as vague as possible. Neal was pretty sure that was because he'd wanted to keep Lori out of it, probably to protect her. *Well, if that was your plan, then it looks like you failed, Dad,* Neal couldn't help thinking. *Not* knowing what was going on might end up being the most dangerous option for Lori since she didn't know who might be after her—meaning danger could come from anywhere. And staring at this vague, half-empty file wasn't doing a damn thing to help Neal protect her.

He sat back and scrubbed a hand over his face, then yawned before glancing over at Lori. After their talk last night, he felt closer to her somehow. It was good and bad. Good, since they needed to work together to solve this thing, and since it would help them maintain their cover story of being a couple. But bad because he didn't want to cross the line with her into anything more than what they had now, regardless of what certain parts of his anatomy felt. She did look cute today though, in that pink top and those black slacks that hugged her curves in all the right places.

Damn.

He needed to get out of this place for a while, get some fresh air and space so he could think clearly again. One of the things he loved most on his SEAL missions was that they were so frequently on the move, out and about, not cooped up in an office somewhere. Neal pushed to his feet and grabbed his jacket from the back of the chair.

"I think I'm going to go over and talk to Ruth directly about what my dad was working on for her. Get a better feel for it." He grabbed his keys and started for the exit, only to be stopped by Lori's voice.

"Wait. I'll come with you," she said. Purse slung over her shoulder, she joined him. "What?"

"Nothing." He blew out a breath. So much for getting some space on his own. "Come on, then."

Once in the car, they headed off toward city center where Ruth's offices were located. As a defense attorney, she definitely had her finger on the pulse of crime in the Detroit metro area. Neal wondered if his dad had somehow gotten caught up in one of her clients' cases. Had his dad found something incriminating on one of her clients that she didn't want to get out? Was that why she'd decided to cancel the investigation? Or did she also believe that her case had resulted in his dad's death? Was that why she'd pulled the plug?

They parked in a garage across from the building where Ruth's offices were located and took the skybridge over. When they arrived, he gave their names to the receptionist and they took a seat in the waiting area. Beige, boring, and bland, just like every other attorney's office he'd ever been in. Before long, a familiar voice greeted them from the hallway nearby. "Neal? Is that you?"

"Hey, Ruth." He stood and hugged her briefly. She was tall and slim with long dark hair she always kept secured neatly in a bun or in a sleek ponytail down her back. Today she was wearing a dark burgundy pantsuit and a warm smile. "How are you?"

"I'm good, thanks. How are you holding up?" She pulled back and gave him a concerned look. "I'm so sorry about your father. I didn't get a chance to tell you the other day at the funeral."

"Thanks. It's been a lot to deal with."

"I'm sure." Ruth glanced past him, her dark brows knitting. "Hey, Lori. What are you doing here?"

"Hi. Um, we had a few questions for you," Lori said, joining them. "Any chance we could talk in your office?"

"Oh, um." Ruth stepped back, looking oddly out of sorts for the first time that Neal could remember. The woman's bread and butter was keeping her cool in difficult situations, so the fact that she seemed nervous now set off all his inner alarm bells. She glanced at the receptionist, then back at them. "My schedule's pretty tight today. I've got another client on the way and—"

"Please," Lori said, stepping closer and lowering her voice. "It's for Gary."

Ruth took a deep breath and gave a curt nod. "Fine. Follow me."

She led them back to her office. "What can I help you with?"

Neal took the lead. "We were wondering if you could tell us about the case my dad was working on for you. I've been going over the case file at the office and it's pretty bare—it doesn't even explain exactly what you had him investigating."

"Right." Ruth fiddled with some papers on her desk, stacking the already neat files there. "Well, there really isn't much to tell, I'm afraid. I had some clients who I asked him to check out because I wasn't sure they were telling me the whole truth." She gave a short chuckle. "Not an unusual occurrence in my line of work. But in this case, a few of my clients had suddenly decided to change their plea to guilty without even discussing it with me. It was unusual and I wasn't sure what to make of it, so I hired Gary to help me find some answers."

"Hmm." Neal crossed his arms, fitting the pieces together in his head. "And did he find anything for you?"

"No." Ruth looked up from her papers. "Honestly, I'm not sure what you're hoping to find out here. Did someone file a complaint against Gary, saying he was harassing them?"

"No, nothing like that," Lori was quick to assure her. "But we wondered if Gary might have made some people angry—in a way that could have led to retaliation."

"What retaliation?" Ruth asked, sounding genuinely confused.

"Surely you're used to people getting angry in your line of work," Neal jumped in. "You probably get threats all the time, right?" He waited to see her reaction to that. She was acting nervous, as if she didn't like the idea of discussing the case, which didn't seem to align with her protests that his father hadn't been able to find anything suspicious. Why would a dead-end case make her this nervous? Had she been getting threats? Had his father?

"Of course," she agreed with a shrug. "Threats are just part of the cost of doing business when you're a lawyer."

"Anonymous threats?" he pressed.

She frowned. "Yes, occasionally. It's mostly just people venting. Sometimes they sign their names, sometimes they don't. People hardly ever act on those threats, so I've learned not to worry about them too much." Her frown deepened. "It wouldn't surprise me to hear that Gary had gotten his share of threats, too—but if he got any in relation to my case, he didn't tell me about them. Are you saying that happened?"

"We can't be sure," Lori answered. "Like we said, he didn't include much in the case file."

"But you think it might have? You're talking as if someone went after Gary." Ruth examined them closely, a worried frown growing on her face. "It almost sounds like you're saying that Gary was murdered… but that can't be right, can it? Wasn't his death ruled a heart attack?"

Neal and Lori exchanged a look. On the drive over, they'd talked about how much information they'd potentially share with Ruth—and the decision had been made to keep it limited. The fewer people who knew they were investigating Gary's death, the better. Lori finally said, "It was. We were just checking in because this case was dropped without being closed, and because Gary's notes on it were so vague. It seemed safest to make sure that there were no unresolved issues that might make trouble for me down the line, now that I'm handling all the investigations myself."

Ruth blinked at them a moment and Neal could practically see the wheels turning in her head, but in the end, she didn't fight them on it. "Right," she said, checking her smart watch and standing. "Well, I'm afraid my next client is due any second, so I'm going to have to cut this short."

She came around the desk and opened the door. Neal and Lori took their cues and rose as well. The goodbyes were quick but courteous before they headed back across the skybridge toward his SUV, talking as they walked.

"Do you think she was acting weird?" Lori asked.

"A little, yeah, especially when we were talking about my dad's case. But I think she was genuinely confused when we brought up the idea that Dad's death could have been tied to her case." He pushed the door open for the parking garage and followed her inside, their voices echoing off the concrete. "Ruth's a good, smart woman. She liked my dad a lot." In the interests of maintaining the truce with Lori, he didn't share his opinion that Ruth had liked Gary more than he'd deserved. He hit the button on his key fob as they neared the SUV, making the lights flash on and off. "If she thought there was any connection between her case and Dad's death, Ruth would've brought it to the police. No way she would've kept that private."

"Hmm. Maybe." Lori climbed into the passenger seat and fastened her seatbelt while Neal did the same behind the wheel. "Unless she was scared."

He looked up at that, considering it a moment before discarding the idea. "She didn't have a noticeable reaction when we asked her about getting threats." He started the engine and pulled out of their spot, heading up the ramp to pay. A pair of headlights switched on behind them as another car pulled out and followed them up the ramp. He paid for their parking, then waited while the stop arm went up and flipped on his turn signal to go right. Neal pulled out onto the street, glancing again in the rearview mirror to see a dark sedan with tinted windows exiting behind them and making the same turn. Huh. Too soon to say they were being tailed, but he was on the alert anyway. They stopped at a red light, then made a left onto a one-way street before making another right.

"Where are you going?" Lori frowned over at him. "This isn't the way back to the office."

"I know." He checked the rearview again and yep. The sedan was still there. Shit. "I think," he said, making another lane change and another right, "that we've picked up a tail."

"Dammit." Lori turned to look out the back window before Neal stopped her. She rested back in her seat, scowling. "You think it's the person who sent me that note?"

"Maybe." They continued on down the street, no more lane changes or turns. "If it is, I don't want to tip them off that we're on to them. But I also don't want to lead them back to the office. So," he took a deep breath. "You hungry?"

She checked her watch. "It's almost noon. I could eat."

"Good." A few miles down the road, they came to a shopping center with a couple of chain restaurants near the front of the lot. They chose the Italian option and Neal parked near the front of the place, keeping an eye on the sedan which pulled around to park along the side. He cut the engine and got out, walking around to Lori's side to hold her door. "They're in the dark sedan five spaces to the left of the dumpster. We need to make them believe we're a couple to sell our story, yeah?"

"Yeah." She took his hand and they headed toward the restaurant.

Neal heard one of the car doors open and acted on instinct, pulling Lori into his arms and kissing her right there on the sidewalk in front of everyone. At first, he kept an eye out over her head to see if he could ID whoever got out of the car, but then slowly the feel of her in his arms, the minty sweet taste of her mouth, became too distracting and he lost himself in the kiss. It was so good. Too good. And by the time they came up for air, the driver of the sedan was gone.

Fuck.

Lori was still blinking up at him, looking as discombobulated as he felt right then. Pulse pounding in his temples and heat sizzling through his body, he managed to open the restaurant door and get her inside even though it was hard to walk, aroused as he was. God, what was it about this woman?

He couldn't afford to lose focus now. There was too much on the line.

While they waited for the hostess to seat them, Lori kept her hand in his, her breath ragged.

"That was…" she said, words shaky. "Wow."

Neal closed his eyes and winced. Lori made him want to let his guard down when what he really needed was to build his barriers up higher and stronger. He needed to keep this professional if they were going to make it out of this alive, literally and figuratively.

7

Once they were seated at a cozy table in the corner, Lori did her best to keep her attention on the enormous menu in front of her and not the man beside her, who'd rocked her world with a single kiss and who now sat close enough that his knee brushed hers constantly under the table.

"What's good here?" he asked, leaning slightly toward her so his warm breath fluttered the hair near her temple, making her shiver.

Lori coughed and frowned at the appetizer page, her stomach too full of butterflies to be hungry. "No idea," she said. "I only picked this one because it shares a bathroom with the other restaurant next door. Figured it would give us an easy out to ditch our tail after we eat."

"Good thinking." He held his menu in one hand, lacing his fingers through hers with the other. Every so often, his gaze flicked up from the menu to scan the room. "Dammit. There's too many people around here for me to say with certainty whether we're being watched or not. There's a couple people on my radar, though."

"Yeah," Lori said, the word emerging more distracted than she wanted. She hated to admit it, because all this—the flirtatious looks, the touches, the whispers, the kiss—Lori knew was part of their cover for the case. None of it was real. But damn if he wasn't turning her on. It had been so long, too long, since anyone had looked at her or touched her like that, and frankly, she was lonely.

That was the excuse she was going with, anyway.

She stared out at the room too, taking in all the local memorabilia on the walls, the 90s soft rock on the stereo system, the smell of grilled meat and veggies in the air. It was a typical chain restaurant that prided itself on celebrating the weekends and friendship. Unfortunately, it was also very popular—and therefore, very crowded. There was just no way to tell if they were being watched or even if someone was listening to what they were saying. Which was probably why Neal had taken care to whisper his words right into her ear. It was *not* so he could send shivers down her spine. Definitely not.

Once the server came, took their orders and brought their drinks, Lori did her best to get her mind out of the gutter and back on track by making small talk. She sipped her sweet tea and asked, "Tell me about growing up in Detroit."

Neal was having none of it, apparently, nuzzling her ear as he asked her more questions about the case. She did her best to focus on his words and not the brush of his lips on her sensitive skin. "Help me understand. What was it about the coffee cup and the wedding ring on the day my dad died that made you so suspicious?"

She took a deep breath to calm her racing pulse and snuggled closer to him, smiling. "I told you already. He never went to that shop. Hated their coffee. And he never took off his ring, so why was it on the floor?"

He sighed and straightened, kissing her hand, the one he was still holding, his thumb tracing lazy patterns on her palm. Talk about the sweetest torture. "I get that it was out of character for him," Neal said, his tone still low and intimate, both to keep up the façade of a date and so even the people in the booth next to them wouldn't be able to hear what they were saying. "I trust your judgment there. I do. But we need to get from that to how those things could have happened. And what do they have to do with his murder? Say he *didn't* buy the coffee —then why was it there?"

"Hmm." Tired of fighting against it, Lori decided to do some torturing of her own. She slipped off her shoe beneath the table and traced her toes up under the hem of his jeans, trailing them up his ankle. Neal stiffened slightly beside her, his hazel eyes going wide, and she couldn't suppress a tiny, wicked smile. Turnabout was fair play, buddy. "Well," she said, matching his tone and sticking close to his side. "Maybe the wedding ring was under the table because Gary was being robbed? Maybe the stress of it brought on the heart attack, and then the thief panicked and ran away?"

Neal cleared his throat and scowled down at the table, his tanned cheeks slightly flushed now. Apparently, she wasn't the only one not totally immune to all this pretend foreplay. Good. She didn't have to suffer alone. His nostrils flared a little as he inhaled deeply. "But nothing else was disturbed. A thief would've demanded that Dad hand over his wallet and phone before they went for his wedding band." His dark brows knit. "Maybe he met someone at the coffee shop for a case earlier that day and they poisoned him in the café?"

Intrigued, Lori picked up that line of thinking. "That's a possibility, definitely. Though I still don't know why he would have actually bought the coffee. You can meet someone at a shop without ordering something there. Or he could have gotten something else—tea or a bottle of water." She slumped. "Or maybe his regular coffee place was too full and the coffee is a red herring?" There was just so much they didn't know. Guessing wasn't the same as finding an actual answer. How would they even know if they were right?

"Or maybe someone brought him that cup of coffee from the wrong shop and it was poisoned," Neal countered.

"I think we need to go to the coffee shop," Lori said, grinning for real this time. Gary might not be able to give them any answers about how he'd ended up with that coffee, but that didn't mean that no one knew. "Talk to the baristas. If we're lucky, they might still have security footage from that day that would show us something."

The server brought their food, and they pulled apart to eat. The pasta was good and the small talk seemed to flow a little better now. Finally, after their meal was finished, Neal paid the bill. (Lori's first instinct was to fight him over it, but seriously. After what he'd pulled with all those kisses and caresses, he deserved to get the tab.) Then they ducked out through the bathrooms, just as she'd suggested.

Of course, once they were back in the car, Neal seemed to flip a switch on his emotions. Went from hot to cold in two seconds flat. And even though she knew rationally that the flirting back at the restaurant had all been pretend, it was still driving her nuts. Because some tiny part of her deep inside still wondered if it had really been all fake. It had seemed so real… And yes, she'd been out of the game a while. Three years to be exact. But that didn't mean she was totally clueless about what real desire looked like in a man's eyes. And she'd seen hints of that in Neal's…hadn't she? As they headed back toward her house, she started to doubt herself. Maybe it was all in her head?

Ugh. What did it matter either way? The last thing she should be thinking about was hooking up with Neal. Because seriously. He wasn't her boss, but he and his brothers had just inherited all of their father's assets, which included the agency she worked for. And after the disaster she went through at her previous job, why the hell was she attracted to someone who could very well torpedo her career yet again?

Idiot.

They took a circuitous route back to her place. The ride was quiet. Neal was never one to start a conversation, and Lori was too wrapped up in her thoughts. When they reached the house, Lori waited for him to punch in the codes for the new, elaborate security system he'd installed in her house, then followed him inside. While he locked the doors behind them and made sure the outside cameras were working, Lori took off her coat, then said she had some things to take care of in her room. She needed some time and space to get her head straight again. She also needed to talk to her best friend about all this—her sister, Alison.

"When you start getting hungry, let me know what you want to do about dinner," she said, lingering at the end of the hallway.

Neal didn't look back at her—just grunted, caveman style.

Perfect.

Lori went to her room and closed the door before picking up her phone and hitting the speed dial for her sister. She felt a little bit like she was going behind Neal's back, calling someone to talk about their investigation and fake relationship when they were doing so much to keep it a secret. But she'd told him from the start that she was going to be honest with her sister. Alison would never believe the "we've been long-distance dating for a year" line anyway—there was no way Lori would have hidden a relationship from her for a year. Besides, Alison already knew about the investigation. They'd talked before about Lori's suspicions regarding Gary's death, and Alison had been the one to encourage her to find someone to help her investigate when the police refused to follow through.

"Hey, sis," Alison said, picking up on the second ring. "What's happening?"

Lori updated her on the situation, then hesitated. "There's a problem, though."

"I'd say so," Alison said.

"I think I might be developing a real crush on my fake bodyguard."

A snort echoed through the phone line. "Okay. Yeah. Sure. SEAL McHottie is hot. Big surprise. Not. Why is you being a normal straight woman getting turned on by a slice of beefcake pie what you're focused on here?" Her sister's voice grew steadily louder as she spoke. "I don't care if his forearms are gorgeous or if he makes the best scrambled eggs in the world. Because what I'm still stuck on is the fact that you received a death threat!"

Lori hung her head. What the hell was wrong with her? Besides the fact she needed to get laid, big time. "I'm sorry. You're right. I'm taking the danger seriously—I promise. But please don't worry about me, okay? Neal's got it under control. He's SEAL trained, and he's been working private security for the past year. He knows what he's doing. And he's also installed a state-of-the-art security system at the house, so nobody's getting in that shouldn't be here."

That seemed to calm Alison down a little, thank goodness. She still had a point when she said, "Well, from now on, when you babysit Hope, I want you to bring her to your highly protected house. I don't care if Neal is there or not. The fact that someone managed to get into the office and leave that note, regardless of the circumstances around it, does not make me feel safe having my daughter there."

"Understood." The conversation was like a bucket of cold water on her inappropriate lust toward Neal. "I completely get that, and if we haven't sorted things out by next week on my babysitting day, I'll tell

Mom to drop Hope off at my house. And thanks for setting me straight. I need to keep my attention on figuring out who killed Gary, not how I feel about my pretend boyfriend who has no intention of sticking around. If Neal can switch off his emotions at the drop of a hat in our fake relationship, then so can I."

8

———————

The next day, after spending a little time in the office, Neal and Lori decided to check out the coffee shop his dad had apparently been at before he died. It was good to have something to think about other than their kiss the day before and all that flirting. Lord knew, Neal had been over and over it in his head through the night enough for the both of them. Subsequently, he'd slept like shit. Tossing and turning, unable to forget the warmth and scent and feel of Lori in his arms, her mouth under his. And then when they'd come into the office, he kept finding his attention drawn to her—to the way the light through the window hit her hair, the way she absent-mindedly hummed a little when she was thinking, or the way he could smell a hint of her perfume across the room. And when she'd gone to get a file out of the back and had bent down to open the cabinet, well…

He'd been more than happy to have a good reason for the two of them to leave. He welcomed the excuse to get outside and walk around in the fresh air for a minute, hoping it would clear his head a little while also giving them the chance to maybe get some answers about the day his father died.

He yanked open the front door to the café with more force than was necessary, sending the bells jangling with a sound far merrier than Neal felt at the moment. It looked like a typical coffee place, with a few people waiting to order or pick up their stuff. They'd deliberately waited until after the morning rush was over, figuring that the staff of the café would be more willing to talk to them if there weren't long lines of customers impatiently waiting to be served. But even during a relative lull, the place still felt cramped and overcrowded, with too many little tables stuffed into too little space and every sound bouncing off the tile walls and tin ceiling to keep the space from ever feeling quiet. The place smelled of fresh-brewed coffee and pretension. No wonder his dad hated it.

"I just can't see Gary coming here," Lori said to him as they got to the back of the line. "I think someone brought him the coffee."

"We can't just assume that," he said, inching forward toward the counter. "We need to prove it."

When someone squeezed past with a tray full of cups, he stepped closer to Lori, putting his hand on her lower back out of an automatic protective instinct. It was a mistake to touch her again, though, because those same damned tingles of awareness zinged up his arm, frustrating the hell out of him. He tried to focus on his job, scanning the cluttered space for any potential threats, but he couldn't turn off his awareness of her warmth right by his side.

Each time they moved a little closer toward the counter, her body brushed against his and he got a whiff of her scent. She smelled good. Too damned good. And why was her shirt so tight? No. Not tight. Just clingy in all the right places.

Fuck. Fuck, fuck, fuck.

Get it together, dumbass.

This is a job, not Dates-R-Us.

"Next!" the barista shouted, and finally they were at the damned counter. Neal swallowed hard and let his hand fall away from Lori's lower back. He'd had it there the whole time? Why the hell had he kept touching her like that? And why hadn't she stopped him?

While he was still trying to work that out in his head, Lori pulled a business card from her purse and slid it over the counter to the barista.

"Hi, my name's Lori Hart and I'm a private investigator," she said, pointing toward the card. "And this is my partner, Neal Ward. We'd like to ask you a few questions for a case we're working on."

"My manager would get on my case if I was just standing around talking to someone who's not a customer," the barista said, her tone flat as a pancake. "If you want me to answer your questions, you're going to have to buy something." Neal blinked at her. She looked to be in her early twenties, black hair, blue eyes, a red bandana wrapped around her head, Rosie the Riveter style.

"Okay, fine," Lori said, pulling out her wallet. "We're ordering." She squinted up at the chalkboard menu behind the counter. "Uh, one skinny chai latte and..." Lori looked up over her shoulder at him. "What do you want, Neal? My treat this time."

"Small black coffee, please," he said, not intending to drink it anyway. "Can you tell us how long you keep surveillance footage of the store? Would you have any from two weeks ago?"

"Nope," the girl said before giving Lori the total for their order.

"No, you don't keep the footage for two weeks?" Neal pressed.

"No, we don't have footage at all," the girl replied, sounding bored to death with the conversation.

"But you have cameras..." Lori said, gesturing to the devices, though now that she mentioned it, Neal could see that the cameras didn't have that red light visible, showing that they were recording.

The girl just shrugged. "They broke back before I even started here, and that was a year ago. The owner's too much of a cheapskate to get the system fixed, so he just leaves them up, saying that as long as people think they're being recorded, they'll behave."

"Were *you* working here on the morning of Tuesday before last?" Neal asked as a last-ditch effort. When the girl nodded, Neal got out his phone and pulled up the most recent picture he had of his dad and passed it over to the barista. "Do you remember if this man was in the café on that morning?"

The barista squinted down at the picture. "Oh no, definitely not. He only came in here once, a few months ago—and he made such a fuss about not liking his coffee that the manager asked him to leave. And then later that day, we saw that he'd posted a one-star review on Yelp. Barry told me that if he came in again, I didn't have to serve him—but he hasn't come back since, thank God."

Lori and Neal stepped to the side to wait for their drinks and to process what they'd been told. On the one hand, it was good news—his dad had been memorable enough that they could be certain he really hadn't been in the coffee shop the morning that he died. The barista definitely would have remembered if he'd returned. But that left them with a slew of unanswered questions. Where did the coffee come from? Who bought it? And was it tampered with in between picking it up from the café and delivering it to Gary's desk?

Finally, their drinks arrived. They collected them, then headed back to the office. On their way in, they dodged a man coming out of the dry cleaners with a load of bags over his shoulder.

"Hi, Kevin," Lori said, waving. "Neal, this is Kevin Murphy. He's the building manager. Kevin, this is my boyfriend, Neal Ward. He's Gary's son."

"Oh, hi," Kevin said, shaking Neal's hand. "I'm sorry for your loss. Nice funeral."

"Thanks." Neal nodded. He didn't recall seeing the guy there, but that day had been a blur. Way too much going on to remember everyone who'd attended. His mind clicked over to the case. "Hey, I'm glad we ran into you today. I wondered how long this building keeps the security footage from these entrance cameras."

"They reset every forty-eight hours." Kevin sounded a little embarrassed. "I know that's not ideal, but other than the dry cleaners here and the gift shop beside it, none of the small businesses in our three-story building keep any cash on hand or have anything worth stealing besides office supplies and paperwork, so it didn't seem worth it to invest in a bigger setup. I mean, the other businesses are an accountant, a divorce attorney and a tiny marketing firm."

"Right." Neal and Lori both gave a disappointed sigh.

"Well, it was worth a try." Lori gave Kevin a bright smile. "Thanks for chatting. Have a good day."

"You too," Kevin said as he headed out the front door with his dry cleaning.

They continued up to the office, Lori's smile fading. "Man, why do we keep hitting dead ends? I feel like I'm failing Gary here."

"You're not failing anybody," Neal assured her, taking the key from her hand and going inside first to do a full office sweep before clearing the space for her to come in. His chest ached slightly at her defeated tone. "Look, we found out more today than you think."

"How so?" she asked, dropping her purse into a drawer at her desk.

"Well, we now know that someone besides my dad must have brought him that coffee. And it was either his murderer or one of the last people to see him alive. Either way, I'd say our next task is to discover who that person is."

"Yeah." Lori slumped down in her chair. "But that just got more difficult without being able to check the building's security footage, so…" She sat back and stared up at the ceiling. "I don't know. Maybe we can ask some of the other businesses in the vicinity. See if they have cameras that might have caught people coming and going from this building and still have the footage available from the morning Gary died." She shook her head and sighed again. "It'll take time, though, to go through all that. And it might not lead to anything."

"True." Neal walked over to his dad's desk and sat down, trying to stay positive. "But if we see anyone involved in one of Gary's cases coming in here that day, then we have a new lead."

She blinked at him a moment, then squared her shoulders and gave a curt nod. "You're right. Let's do it. It's a good idea. And I'll start researching poisons that could be mixed into coffee and mimic the symptoms of a heart attack, or that could somehow trigger a heart attack."

"Good." Neal popped the lid off his coffee and took a tentative sip, then spit it out. Yep. Tasted like shit warmed over. "Yuck. Dad was right. This is awful."

She tipped her chai tea latte at him and winked. "See? You and your dad have something in common after all."

9

The rest of the day passed by pretty uneventfully. Lori spent most of her time on the computer, handling the work for her current case load, and Neal went over more old case files, looking for clues as to who might have wanted his dad dead. While the two of them agreed that it was most likely this was somehow connected to Ruth's case, they'd also decided that it wouldn't hurt to cover their bases and check on old cases as well, to see if Gary's case notes included mention of any threats or attempts to harm him. There was always a chance that the killer was someone from the investigator's past, maybe even a person Gary had helped get arrested and sent to jail who had since gotten released, and who had tracked Gary down for some overdue revenge.

But since Neal hadn't called her over to look at anything—and, in fact, looked like he was on the verge of nodding off a couple of times —Lori was pretty sure he hadn't found anything promising, or even particularly interesting. Being a private investigator sounded glamorous when it was an old black-and-white movie with Humphrey Bogart, but in real life, it tended to be pretty dull.

Around four-thirty, his cell phone rang, and while Lori did her best not to eavesdrop on the conversation, it was kind of hard not to with them both being in one big room and all. She could only hear one side, of course, but from what she gathered, Neal was talking to his older brother, Lance, and he wasn't too happy about it.

When he finally hung up, she took one look at Neal's sour expression and winced. "Everything okay?"

It took him a minute to respond, like he was lost in his thoughts or something, just staring down at his phone. Then he looked up, those walls sliding back into place as he shoved his phone back into his pocket. "Yeah. Everything's fine. That was my brother. He wants us to swing by the house tonight, so I can go through my old stuff and see what I want to keep, if anything. I tried to tell him that I couldn't, because I need to stick close to you and keep you safe, but he said to bring you along, so…"

"That's fine." She stood and collected her purse from her drawer. "We can go now, if you want. It's a little early, but I don't have anything left on my schedule that has to get done today."

He looked about as enthusiastic as a root-canal patient, but sometimes you had to do hard things, especially when it came to family.

They locked up and headed out to the car, making the short drive from the office to Gary's old house. Once they arrived, Lance led them upstairs to what was apparently Neal's old room, and Lori had to bite back a grin. It was exactly how she'd pictured a young Neal's space—full of toys and books and old sports posters. It was pretty obvious that he hadn't been back in years, so the place was a sort of time capsule for the Neal-that-was.

"Wow," she said, standing in the doorway with Lance while Neal wandered inside. "Looks like you were really into the Lions."

Neal shrugged, looking around like he was staring at blocks of wood and not treasured childhood mementos. Lori was a bit taken aback by that. She got that he had issues with his dad, but she didn't think his childhood had been *all* bad. His brothers were a part of it, after all, and they seemed to have a good relationship. Instead of being sad or nostalgic, though, Neal just looked irritated that he had to be there at all.

Hoping to defuse the tense situation, she reached over and picked up a board game from a nearby shelf. "Oh wow. I used to love this game. Alison and I would always fight over who got to be green."

"Yes!" Ryan said, nudging in between her and Lance. "Remember when we used to play this, bro? You always won and I knew you were cheating."

"I never cheated," Neal said, chuckling at last. He walked over to them. "I was four years older than you, bud. Of course I was going to win."

"Whatever." Ryan shook his head. "Overconfident much?"

"Always."

Neal grinned and it was like the sun coming out from behind the clouds for Lori. He headed over to the bookshelf, and his smile grew softer as he ran his finger down the spine of a battered copy of *Treasure Island.* "Remember when you used to read this to us at bedtime?" he asked, turning to Lance.

"Biggest mistake of my life," Lance teased with a theatrical groan.

"Why's that?" Lori asked, eager to keep the warm, nostalgic mood going.

"Because these two idiots decided that they wanted to be pirates, and for the next month, I never knew when they would mount their next expedition to steal all the treasure in the house."

"Treasure?" Lori looked to Neal.

"Basically anything shiny," he admitted. "Things got a little dicey when we stole all the silverware and refused to give up the booty. Lance had to run to the store and get some plastic forks, or we would have had to eat spaghetti that night with our hands." The three brothers chuckled, and Lori couldn't help joining in. "And I have to admit," Neal added, directing the words to Lance, "I honestly don't remember what I did with your keychain. Did you ever end up finding it?"

"Yes," Lance groaned. "*Two weeks later,* after I'd already paid to have all my keys recut. Man, you two were pains in the ass."

"Hey, don't look at me," Ryan piped in. "I was just the cabin boy— Neal was the pirate captain."

"You didn't take turns?" Lori asked.

Ryan looked a little sheepish. "It was years later before I realized that was an option. Neal told me he was the captain, so I just believed him. I didn't know that little brothers could ever be in charge."

It was fun to see the three brothers' happiness as they talked about the past. But then a moment later, Neal picked up what looked like a stuffed bear. Or maybe a moose. Hard to tell with most of the fur gone and only one eye. Whatever it was, it caused the smile to drop off his face in an instant.

"Dude! Is that Mr. Moto?" Ryan asked, laughing. "I can't believe Dad kept all this stuff."

"Dad kept everything," Lance said, leaning against the doorframe looking contemplative. "I remember when he gave that to you, Neal. It was right after our mom died. You carried that thing around like it was another appendage. Took it everywhere with you."

"Aw, he's cute," Lori said, hoping to make him smile again. "And I bet he was your favorite too, based on how he looks, all loved to bits."

Those stern walls around Neal suddenly crashed down and he tossed the old bear away like he'd been burned. "I don't want it. I don't want any of it. Give it all away. Get rid of it. I don't care."

He stalked out of the room and downstairs, the front door slamming behind him with a resounding *thwack*, leaving the rest of them to stare after him, stunned.

Ryan shook his head and turned away, heading back down the hall to what Lori assumed was his old room. She stood there a moment with Lance, feeling torn and twisted inside. There was one thing, though, that Lori was certain of.

"Hey," she said, placing a hand on Lance's arm. "Don't get rid of all of this yet, okay? I know what he said, but he's going through a lot right now. Let me talk to him and we'll come back when he's in a better frame of mind."

Lance gave a curt nod and Lori headed back downstairs to meet Neal in the car. In the end, they didn't say much on the way home. Neal spent the drive brooding quietly to himself and Lori spent it staring out the windows, not sure what to do. It was obvious he was having a hard time with his dad's death, but for whatever reason he wouldn't talk about it, wouldn't admit it, even to himself.

When they finally got home, they took off their coats, and then she went into the kitchen to stick another frozen pizza into the oven. For once, Neal didn't object and offer to cook for them, which was yet another signal that he was seriously upset. She got a couple of beers out of the fridge, set the timer on the pizza, then went back into the living room to find Neal on the sofa, staring blankly across the room at the images on the TV.

"Hey," she said, handing him a beer, then curling into the corner of the sofa across from him. "How about we forget the case for tonight. Why don't we just relax and eat and maybe watch a movie together?"

Neal didn't respond.

"Want to talk about what's bothering you?" she hazarded.

"No."

Great. They were back to monosyllabic again.

"You know," she said, after sipping her beer, "I know we promised to be professional when we're not keeping up the dating act around other people, but that doesn't mean we can't be friends too and—"

"Jesus!" He pushed to his feet, anger flushing his cheeks. "I said I don't want to talk about it, all right? It's none of your business. I'm your bodyguard here, not your boyfriend. Not your friend. Got it?"

She did her best to hide the rush of hurt clawing inside her and stinging her eyes, but apparently didn't do a good job of it because Neal cursed under his breath, then stormed off down the hall to the bathroom, where he closed the door and locked it behind him.

Blinking hard, she did her best not to cry and failed. God, she really was an idiot. An idiot who mistook his pretending for the real thing, and how pathetic did that make her? How needy, that she was actually looking to her fake boyfriend to give her affection.

Well, Lori wasn't pathetic, and she was done with this mind-fuck shit. Neal wanted to wallow in his anger and pain over his dad? Fine, let him. He obviously didn't want her help, and she was through offering it to someone who didn't appreciate the gesture.

Resolute, she headed down the hall herself to change before the pizza was done. She didn't know if Neal would join her or not, but at the moment, she didn't much care.

10

The following night, Neal sat in his car, parked across the street from the building that housed the Ward Investigation offices, and watched the people on the sidewalk. Lori was upstairs on the top floor, still working on her current case load. She was making quick progress through the cases that were still on her docket. He'd caught the nervous looks she kept giving her dwindling inbox as she made her way through another one of the last projects the firm had contracted when his father was still alive. It was clear that she wasn't sure what would happen when the current case load ran out. But in the meantime, she was giving those cases everything she had. He'd over-heard one phone call she'd gotten that day where a client had praised her for the excellent work she had done. He'd been watching her out of the corner of his eye, as he did practically all the time now, and had waited for her to turn to him, to share her good news, to let him congratulate her. Yeah, he didn't need to actually be told because he'd picked up on most of it just from hearing her side of the conversation, but he still wanted to give her the chance to brag, to share her joy.

But she hadn't. She'd looked over at him, and then her face had fallen. Without saying a word, she'd turned back to her desk and her work, which she'd continued in silence. That had been the theme of the day. Strained, awkward silence. That was the real reason why he was out here, sitting in his car. It sure as hell wasn't to enjoy the scenery. Downtown Detroit could seem bleak even on the best of days, and right now it was chilly and cloudy, which matched Neal's mood to a T. But at least out here, he had some distance from Lori—and could pretend he was doing something useful. Going through his dad's files ad nauseam hadn't turned up anything useful, so he'd decided it might be helpful to surveil the neighborhood, get a sense for the comings and goings from this building and the other buildings nearby.

He sighed and shifted slightly in his seat, watching a guy and his dog pass the building's entrance. So far, he hadn't seen anyone who looked even remotely threatening go near the place. Plus, it was nine p.m., well after business hours, and the building was locked up tight, except for his dad's office.

Neal angled back so his weight leaned against the car door behind him and propped a foot up on the center console, settling in for what would probably prove to be a long, boring night until Lori was finally ready to drive home. A drive that would probably also be spent in strained, awkward silence.

Things were… not good between them, and it was his fault. He hadn't meant to be so harsh toward her the other night when she'd tried to talk to him about his dad. But dammit, he couldn't focus on the case and her at the same time. And after going back to the house and seeing all his old stuff?

Well, he was just too raw to deal with any of it at that point.

It unsettled him, being back in the house, back among his own things. When he thought of his childhood, he tended to remember the bad parts. Or if he thought of any of it with fondness, it would be the parts that revolved around his brothers. Neal hadn't quite been sold on the idea of a little brother when Ryan was a baby who didn't do much aside from sleep and poop, but once he started walking and talking, Neal had quickly come to relish having a shadow who followed him around all the time and thought everything he did was amazing. And while Neal might never say this out loud, Lance was just about the best big brother imaginable. At seven years older than Neal—eleven years older than Ryan—he'd been the one who had all but raised them until they were old enough to look after themselves. Little wonder they'd both followed in his footsteps, joining the navy and becoming SEALs. Lance had been their ideal for what a grown-up should be— strong, capable, reliable, strict but fair, occasionally exasperated but always loving. It was easy to look up to Lance. It was a hell of a lot harder to look up to his dad, who had let them all down over and over again.

But being home reminded him that there had been good moments too. Moments when his dad had tried to be a good father. Still in his bedroom was the "big boy bed" he remembered Dad and Lance putting together for him—Dad cursing like a sailor when he acciden-tally slammed the hammer on his thumb. The baseball glove his dad had bought him for Christmas the year he really got into the Tigers. The closet Dad would check for monsters any time Neal asked. Even the bedroom door that creaked a little—a sound he remembered from when Dad would get home late and sneak in to kiss his forehead and make sure he was tucked in safe and warm. He'd been a shitty father in a lot of ways, but he'd been a loving father in plenty of ways, too. It twisted something inside Neal to remember that, because for better or for worse, his dad was gone now, and there would be no chance to make any more memories.

Being home again only kept those open wounds from healing. And if he added in his completely ill-advised attraction to Lori and the way *that* was twisting him in knots, well…

God. What the actual fuck am I doing?

He raked a hand through his hair, then fiddled with the zip on his jacket, scowling.

Truth was, he had no clue.

All he knew was that last night, when Lori had asked him if he'd wanted to talk about what was upsetting him, he'd actually wanted to tell her. Worse, if they weren't working on this case together, and she didn't work for his dad's old agency, and he wasn't going back to Cleveland as soon as this whole mess was over, she'd have been exactly the kind of woman he'd fall for.

"Shit," he muttered, shaking his head.

This was getting him exactly nowhere.

Movement caught his attention and his gaze flicked up to the alley beside the building. It was dark and hard to tell, but yeah. There was definitely someone there, near the side door. Neal straightened in his seat and leaned forward to peer more closely at the figure. That was when he smelled the smoke.

For a second, he was too stunned to do anything. Then he fell back on muscle memory and rote. Situations like this were exactly what the SEALs trained for over and over and over again. Why they kept drilling until the teams could handle a crisis in their sleep. Because when a training scenario became reality and the adrenaline flooded your system, there was no time to think or hesitate. You needed to act. Now.

Neal pulled out his cell phone and dialed 911 even as he climbed out of the SUV, and ran towards the building as he gave the address to the operator and requested fire trucks, ASAP. Now that the tree wasn't blocking his line of sight anymore, he had a clear view of their office windows. No signs of fire were visible yet, but the smoke smell was heavier now. He flinched when he looked at the fire escape, remembering how Lori had told him that it was unsafe, but that the building owner was dragging his feet on getting it repaired. She wouldn't have that exit route as an option.

He headed straight for the alleyway and the side door he'd seen the figure emerge from. The alley was empty now, of course, but the door was still cracked open. He headed inside and climbed the stairs there two at a time. The higher he went, the thicker the smoke became, clogging his throat and stinging his eyes. He pulled the collar of his T-shirt up over his nose and mouth and continued climbing. This was bad. Very bad. And it was spreading far too fast and was far too big for a simple electrical fire. Nope. He'd bet good money someone had intentionally started it.

His thoughts flew back to the figure in the alley, then quickly diverted to the woman trapped on the top floor. Lori. Fuck, fuck, fuck. The words hit with every pound of his footsteps on the stairs.

Please don't let me be too late. Please God.

Once he reached the third floor, he slammed out of the stairwell into the hallway and nearly choked. Black smoke clung to the ceiling like a sinister ghost and there! Across the way, the door to the office. It had been blocked from the outside. Barricaded with a bunch of old office furniture and boxes that had been set on fire.

Outside, the wail of sirens grew closer, signaling the imminent arrival of the fire department, but Neal knew there was no time to waste. He had to get her out of there immediately.

He ran over to the towering pyre and screamed over the roar of the flames. "Lori! Lori are you in there? Can you hear me? Lori?"

A beat ticked by. Two. Each seeming to take forever. Until, finally, there was a cough, then an answering call. "Yes! I'm here. I'm okay." More coughing. "But I can't get out. The door won't open."

The fire was moving fast now. Based on Neal's training and experience, he didn't think they'd have time to wait for the fire department to make it up here. But even if he could somehow get all that burning shit out of the way and get the door open, he feared the fire could rush in and burn Lori alive.

Shit.

Okay. Think, Ward. Think.

He needed another way in, one that didn't involve the flaming door. Neal ran through the schematics of the floor layout and realized that there was an empty office space next door to theirs, one that shared a wall with Ward Investigation. Squinting through the hazy air, Neal made his way there, and managed to rip a small fire extinguisher off the wall along the way. It would do little to douse the raging inferno now covering the office's door, but that might serve another purpose. After smashing through the glass entry doors of the office next door, Neal crawled inside and raced back to the shared wall, using all his strength to bash a hole in it with the fire extinguisher. Lori must have realized what he was doing, because she started working on her side of the wall too. Soon they had a space large enough for her to crawl through. She was coughing and bruised, her eyes red and streaming with tears, but damn if seeing her alive and well wasn't the best thing he'd seen in years. Maybe ever.

"You okay?" he asked, taking her hand.

"Been better," she said, giving a little snort. "Let's get out of here."

They made it downstairs just as the fire department arrived and raced past them to get inside the building.

11

"Someone barricaded her in," Neal said to one of the police officers who were taking their statements while Lori got checked out by an EMT on scene.

Barricaded me in.

Lori still couldn't quite wrap her head around that. She'd almost died tonight. Would have died, horribly and alone, if Neal hadn't been there to save her.

"I was doing surveillance on the building from my SUV across the street." He pointed to it. "I saw someone leaving from the side service entrance to the building. Right before I smelled smoke."

The fire. The threatening note. They were tied together. They had to be. This couldn't have been an accident or a misunderstanding. She'd been targeted deliberately, by someone who wanted her to die. Someone who had already killed her friend and mentor. And she still had no idea who that might be.

"Ouch!" she said as the EMT dabbed antiseptic on a cut to her forehead. The pain snapped her out of her thoughts and she leaned around the guy tending to her to tell the cop, "There's a convenience store catty-corner from the alley. Their security cameras should have caught footage of that alleyway. You guys should check that out. If you'll share what you find with me, I can let you know if I recognize the arsonist."

The cop nodded to her and scribbled something on the tiny notepad in his hand. "Okay. Thanks, folks. I think that's all the questions I have for now. We'll be in touch if we're able to get anything useful off those security cameras. And if you remember anything else, anything that might help you identify the person responsible, please let me know."

The EMT moved Lori back in front of him and put some steri-strips across her cut. "Ma'am, I strongly advise that you let us take you to the hospital to be checked out. We can't be sure if you strained your lungs with the smoke inhalation, and there may be other problems from the fire that they need to screen you for. You're running on adrenaline right now, and that could be masking some serious issues."

"No." Lori dug her heels in. She was exhausted and a bit sore from everything she'd been through, but otherwise fine. She just wanted to go home and shower away the smell of smoke, and then get into her bed and sleep for several days. Or maybe years. Once the EMT was done treating her, she slid off the back bumper of the ambulance and handed the guy back his blanket. "Thank you for your help, but I'm fine. Really. Is there something I need to sign to waive your liability for me or whatever?"

"Yeah." The EMT shook his head, then rifled around for a clipboard and pen. "Sign here and here." He pointed at the paper, then looked over at Neal. "You going to stay with her tonight?"

Neal nodded.

"Good. If you notice her having any difficulty breathing, any shortness of breath, wheezing, coughing, dark colored mucus, or changes to her mental state, like restlessness or agitation or confusion or extreme fatigue, get her to the ER right away."

"Will do," Neal said. "I was trained in basic medic skills in the SEALs."

The EMT shook Neal's hand. "Thanks for your service, man."

"You too," Neal said. Then he wrapped an arm around Lori's shoulders and led her to the truck, where he bundled her inside and took her home.

As they drove, Lori did her best to suppress the aftereffects of the trauma she'd just been through—the shaking, the chills, the tears she didn't dare let fall. She didn't want to fall apart in front of Neal. She wanted him to think of her as capable and strong, but…man, it was hard to feel strong when she couldn't stop trembling. So she stared out the window without really seeing anything at all except that black smoke creeping under the door, ever closer to her. The coldness of the windows pressed to her back and the heat in the room as it grew higher and higher. The piercing wail of the smoke alarm on the wall and knowing that she could very well die before anyone even knew she was in danger….

"Why didn't you call me for help as soon as you realized the fire had started?" Neal demanded as they pulled into her driveway a short time later. His voice sounded as rough as she felt, and through the eerie green glow of the dashboard lights, she saw his tortured expression. "If only you'd called me, I could've gotten there sooner, Lori. Gotten you out before…" He waved a hand in her direction before slamming it against the steering wheel and cursing under his breath. "It didn't have to get so bad."

Blinking hard against the sting in her eyes, she stared down at her hands in her lap, toying with the hem of her shirt to hide the tremor in her fingers. "I don't know," she whispered, telling the truth. "It all happened so fast, Neal. It's not like I consciously decided *not* to call you. In the moment, I wasn't really thinking at all. I'm used to just having myself to rely on and my first instinct was to try and escape, not wait for some knight in shining armor to come rescue me."

He didn't say anything, just stared straight ahead at her garage door in front of them and cut the engine. Silence blanketed the car, and the headlights flickered off, leaving them in darkness. She couldn't tell if it was a blessing or a curse, so she continued, the space feeling oddly intimate now.

"I kept trying to open the door, but by the time I realized it was blocked, it was already too hot to touch. I did consider taking my chances with that old fire escape, but…while I was still working up my nerve to try it, I heard you calling my name and breaking down the wall to get to me. After that, my only thought was to find something to help you make a hole." She shrugged.

Neal sat back and exhaled slowly, his profile outlined by moonlight. "We're a team, Lori. Being open and communicating works both ways, you know."

"I know," she said, staring out the window beside her again.

"I can do my job of protecting you better if you trust me," he continued, his tone softer now. "What happened back there tonight, it was too close a call, Lori. I need you safe." Neal inhaled deeply, unsnapped his seatbelt, then shifted to face her in the shadows, intensity coming off him in waves. "I lied to you last night, Lori." Her heart skipped. "When I told you that you weren't my friend, that I was just your bodyguard—that wasn't true at all." He hung his head and she had to clench her fists to keep from reaching for him. "That's how it probably *should* be, us being strictly professional here, but dammit." Neal propped one arm on the back of her seat and stared out the rear window of the truck, close enough now for his warmth to envelop her, chase away the chill in her soul. His breath stirred the hair near her temple and she closed her eyes. "The truth is, I care about you, Lori. More than I should. And I need you to trust me here because I need you to be safe. Understand?"

Maybe it was the trauma of the near-death experience she'd had earlier. Maybe it was the fact that she was tired, so tired of being alone. Maybe it was fate. Whatever it was, she couldn't lie to him. Not tonight. Not anymore. So she gave him the truth. "I do trust you, Neal." She took a deep breath and pushed onward before she couldn't anymore. "The second I heard your voice back there in the office, I knew I was going to be okay. Because you were there. Because I knew you'd take care of me, that you'd find a way to save me, no matter what." She relaxed her hands, unfastened her own seatbelt, then reached over, tentatively, to cup his cheek. She noticed her hand wasn't trembling anymore. What she was feeling now was enough to push back the fear. "I care about you too. Way more than I should."

The air between them began to sizzle with promise. For a moment, time slowed. Neal blinked at her, his eyes glittering in the shadows. Then he leaned in and kissed her. Not like the last time, where it had been all for show. Nope. This time it was warm and sweet and tender, a brush of lips once, twice, before they settled on hers. Tasting. Testing. Then things quickly grew more passionate as she gasped beneath him and he took advantage, sweeping his tongue into her mouth as his arms wrapped around her, hauling her up against him. The heat of him was searing, but where the fire back in the office had terrified her, this heat couldn't have been more welcome. It burned through the chill of loneliness and uncertainty, making her feel cherished and desired. *Very much* desired.

Except the truck wasn't cooperating and the center console got in the way. They broke apart, both chuckling slightly as Lori rubbed her sore hip.

"I think maybe we should take this inside," she said, her forehead resting against his.

"Agreed." Neal's breath fanned her face and his smile shone bright in the darkness. "Let's go."

12

The walk from the driveway to the porch passed in a blur for Neal. Then they were at the door and his heart was pounding so hard and so loud that he'd swear it would wake up the entire neighborhood. He managed to get the key in the lock after several failed attempts because he was just too damned revved up. Then they were inside. An awkward moment passed, where they both hesitated, then Lori was on him like white on rice.

Neal barely got the door closed before she was back in his arms, her hands locked behind his neck and her legs around his waist as she kissed him for all she was worth. He surrendered completely, so ready and willing for this. He needed her. More than he'd needed anybody in a long time. Maybe ever.

They stumbled down the short hall and into her bedroom. Neal let her slide to the floor in front of him, then tore off his jacket and shirt, tossing them aside without caring where they landed before sinking his fingers into her silken dark hair and kissing her deep and hot again. He couldn't get enough of her. Would never get enough of her.

Lori, too, seemed desperate for him, kissing and licking every inch of skin he'd exposed, taking extra time to toy with his sensitive nipples, making him shudder against her. It had been a long time since he'd been with anyone, first because of his tours of duty, then because he was recovering from the injuries that had forced his discharge. But tonight, there was only the two of them, only this, right here, right now, and he wanted to make it last forever.

She'd kissed her way down his chest to his pecs and farther down, following the trail of dark hair that led down the middle of his abdomen and disappeared beneath the waistband of his jeans. His cock felt hard as granite, blood thumping in time with his pulse, and if he didn't stop this, didn't focus on something other than how good it felt to have her touch him, this would all be over too soon. So he summoned his willpower and gently pulled her away and up, so Lori stood before him once more.

They hadn't turned on any lights yet, and that was fine by him. He didn't need her seeing all his scars and battle wounds. Didn't want to see the disappointment in her eyes, or worse—pity. Nope. Right now, he just wanted her naked and beneath him, around him, calling out his name as he made her come so hard her toes curled and the angels sang.

First, though, he needed her out of those clothes.

He slipped his hands beneath the hem of her shirt and tugged it up over her head, leaving her in just her bra from the waist up. The fabric still smelled of smoke from the fire and the ache in his chest tightened. He could have lost her tonight. Could have missed out on the chance to ever have this time with her and frankly, that would have killed him too. He leaned in to kiss her, slipping his hands behind her back to unhook her bra, letting the straps slide slowly down her arms until she was naked before him. Then he just looked. The clouds from earlier had disappeared, apparently, because there was enough moonlight streaming now in through the gauzy curtains to bathe her in a hazy, ethereal light. Slowly, he reached up and cupped her breasts, stroking his thumbs over her taut nipples, and she moaned low in her throat, nearly undoing him right there. Then he knelt and took first one, then the other nipple in his mouth, licking and sucking until she clutched his hair, holding him close like she'd never let him go.

Then he went lower, kissing his way down her quivering abdomen to the top of her jeans. He rested his forehead against her belly as he undid her pants, unzipping them slowly and pulling them down her legs until she was left in just her panties. Her scent intoxicated him, soap and sweet arousal, and just a hint of smoke from the fire, reminding him again and again how precious and vulnerable and easily lost all of this was. It was too much. It wasn't enough. He nuzzled her through the lace of her thong, nudging her thighs wider and loving her with his mouth and fingers until her knees buckled and he caught her in his arms. He lifted her up, ready to put her on the bed, but she stopped him.

"Wait," Lori said. "I want to see you."

Before he knew it, she'd reached over and flipped the bedside light on and Neal froze.

Her gaze slowly traveled from his face downward, and his heart sank along with it. Wasn't like he was a monster or something, but the accident had left him with lasting reminders of his sacrifice. He'd do it all again, in a heartbeat, to save his teammates—but he dreaded the thought of the rejection he might face now.

"Oh, wow," she said, tracing her fingertips over his left torso, making him shiver. They'd long since stopped hurting, at least physically. He set her down and she stood before him, gentle compassion filling her eyes as she stared at him. "Oh, Neal. What happened to you?"

Shit. He turned away, throat tight. "IED explosion during the war. Me and my SEAL team were heading into Kandahar for a mission. I was driving and noticed something not right on the road ahead. By the time I realized what it was it was too late, we were already on it. So I swerved the Humvee at the last minute so my door took the bulk of the blast."

"You saved your teammates' lives," she whispered, her tone drenched in awe.

He shrugged, still uncomfortable with all the attention he'd gotten for it. "I was just doing my job, being a good friend and squad mate. They would've done the same for me."

"You're a hero," Lori said, taking his arm and turning him around to face her once more before leaning in and kissing each one of his scars before rising up on tiptoe to kiss his lips. "My hero. I need you, Neal. So badly I hurt."

There was something about how she said it—*I need you, Neal*—that lit him up inside like a firework. Maybe because he needed her too, more than he needed his next breath. "I need you too, Lori."

Then they were back on each other, hot and heavy and oh so right. They tumbled together onto the bed and her panties and his jeans and boxers disappeared in a flurry of kisses and nips and all kinds of stroking. Once they were finally skin to skin, Neal rolled over so she was on her back and licked his way down her body again, tasting her and making love to her again with his mouth and fingers until she was boneless and sated beneath him. He finally rose up and fumbled through his balled-up jeans on the floor for a condom before putting it on and returning to her side on the bed. Any doubts he'd had earlier about her not wanting him because of his scars were long gone now, as she looked at him with blatant desire in her pretty blue eyes. His cock felt ready to burst as it was and he gripped himself tight as he poised above her, his tip at her wet entrance, to stem the inevitable tide inside him. Finally, he sank into her in one long thrust, then held still. She was so tight and hot and… "God, you feel incredible."

"You too," she said, then arched beneath him, pulling his head down for an open-mouthed kiss. Lori locked her ankles behind his lower back and Neal set up a rhythm that soon had them both teetering on the edge of orgasm. Tension coiled at the base of his spine and his balls tightened and it wouldn't be long at all. He reached between them and stroked her slick folds, his thumb circling her most sensitive flesh, and Lori cried out as her body milked him through her third—or maybe fourth—orgasm. Either way, it was more than Neal could take. He thrust into her once, twice more, then came hard inside her, his world going white and fuzzy with pleasure.

Afterward, long afterward, when they'd cleaned up and put on pajamas and gotten back into bed, they lay together in the soft glow of the lamplight, Neal on his back and Lori snuggled into his side. His mind kept circling back to the fact that someone had tried to kill her tonight. And he'd been down in his car, very nearly too far away to stop it.

No. He couldn't let that happen again. Time to face the fact that he couldn't keep Lori safe enough all by himself. He needed backup. He needed his brothers. He didn't want to ruin the mood by talking murder after sex, but this was too important to wait. "I think it's time we tell my family the truth, about the case."

"Really?" Lori frowned, propping herself up on an elbow to look at him. "What changed your mind?"

He sighed. "Tonight. I think we need to get their help on this. I also think we need to tell the police about the threatening note. With the arson attempt, it's clear that whoever is doing this knows you're investigating. There's no reason to keep our investigation secret anymore. We need all the help we can get."

Lori seemed to take that in a second, then nodded, resting her head on his chest, right over his heart. "Okay. You're right. We tell them tomorrow."

Neal reached over and flipped off the light, slipping his arm beneath his head on the pillow. He'd been thinking of other things too. Things like maybe convincing Lori to leave PI work behind. If she did, then they could have a normal life together when this was all over. Cleveland wasn't really that far from Detroit. She could move down there with him and still be within a few hours' drive of her family for visits. She could find another job that satisfied her urge to help people, something that wouldn't consume her life the way being a private investigator did. Something that would allow her to have the kind of home life his father had never been able to have—with him, and maybe some kids someday.

Not that they were there yet, but it still circled in his mind, lingering there.

He stroked her hair until her breath evened out into the patterns of sleep. Neal stayed awake a while longer, savoring the brief moments of peace he felt here, with her, before finally drifting off himself.

13

———

Loud banging woke Lori up around noon the next day. She cracked one eye open and groaned as the sound of Neal letting her mother and Hope into the house echoed down the hall. Moments later, her mom burst into the bedroom without knocking.

"I saw the fire on the news this morning, sweetie," her mom said, looking more frantic than Lori had ever seen her. "When I couldn't get ahold of you on your phone, I panicked and raced over here, hoping you were okay. Why didn't you call me?"

"Well, I…uh…" Before she could answer, Hope ran in and jumped on the bed, hugging Lori tight.

"I'm glad you're okay, Auntie," Hope said, her face smushed in Lori's chest.

It was so sweet, Lori's heart ached. She squeezed her niece back hard, then pulled back. "I'm sorry I scared you, snugglebug."

"I'm just glad you're okay," her mom said, sniffling. "I was so worried."

80

"Aw, Mom." Then Lori was hugging her too, feeling cared for and loved. She let her mom go and put an arm around Hope, pulling the little girl into her side. "Thanks for caring."

"And to answer your question," Neal said from near the doorway, "she's been sleeping. That's why she didn't call. Her body probably needed it after the adrenaline of last night."

Heat prickled Lori's cheeks as she remembered not just the fire, but what had happened afterward. All the things they'd done right here in her bed. Oh my.

Her mother, far too perceptive for her own good, did a quick look between them both and raised a knowing brow at Lori.

Much as she wanted to keep last night to herself, at least a little longer, to savor those memories, better to hit this head-on and be done with it. Lori sent Hope out to the living room to play with the toys Lori kept for her there, after a final kiss to the top of her head. Then she straightened, resting back against the headboard as she waved Neal farther into the room and told him to close the door.

"Uh, actually, Lori," he said, looking uncomfortable as hell, "I was just about to wake you up before they got here. We need to get downtown to the police station by one o'clock." At her questioning look, he added, "I called this morning and made the appointment for us to talk to someone and follow up our statements from last night."

Her mother's expression shifted from suspicious to confused in under a second. "Sweetie, what exactly is going on here?"

Lori took a deep breath and nodded, glancing at Neal and back to her mother. "We need to come clean to you, Mom. Neal and I haven't been dating. That was our cover story, to hide the fact that he's actually been helping me with an investigation."

Her mother's eyes narrowed. "Is this about Gary?"

Looked like her mom was putting that mother-mind reader thing to use. "Yeah," she admitted. "I've never believed his death was natural—and I'm even more sure of that now. The fire was set deliberately, blockading me in the office, to make me stop digging." When her mother gasped in horror, Lori was quick to reassure her that Neal was very qualified to keep her safe and had, in fact, saved her life the previous night.

"And we're going to be getting more backup," Lori promised. "That's why we're going to talk to the police—and later, we'll be sharing everything with Neal's brothers. They're both Navy SEALs. Anyway, I'll fill you in on the rest later." She gave her mom a hug, grabbed some clothes out of the dresser, and then headed for the bathroom where the shower was calling her name.

The last thing she saw before she closed the door was her mother looking at Neal with far more warmth than Lori had ever seen prior to then. So maybe telling her the truth, at least part of it, was a good thing.

She took a quick shower and dressed. Lori was part way through drying her hair when a quick knock rang through the room. She switched off her hairdryer and opened the door. Neal stood there, showered and dressed as well, leaning against the doorframe with one shoulder, and her pulse stumbled despite her wishes. They were in work mode now, not sexy time.

Focus, girl.

Lori cleared her throat and turned away fast, scrambling to get her thoughts back on track and out of the gutter. She concentrated on applying a quick touch of mascara to her lashes instead. "What's up?"

He held up two new phones, one in each hand. "I called Ryan and had him pick these up this morning. He dropped them off an hour or so ago."

"You told them about the fire?" she asked, her gaze flicking to his in the mirror.

"Yeah. They still think it's a stalker, though, not anything to do with Dad's death. Not yet. That felt like it should be an in-person talk." His words hung there a second before he continued. "Anyway." He held up one of the phones again. "This one is to replace the one you lost last night in the fire, at least until you get a good replacement." He set it on the counter, then held up the second phone, which was noticeably smaller. "And this one is for emergencies. You keep it on you at all times. Not in a purse that you might put down or leave behind—physically on your body. No exceptions. I don't ever want another situation where you can't get ahold of me if you need me. Understood?"

She stepped back and faced him, frowning. "What if I don't have pockets?"

"Then shove it in your bra," he said, crossing his arms, his tone stern. "I'm serious, Lori. No excuses. You need to keep it on and with you at all times."

"Okay." She shoved it into the pocket of her jeans, then returned to the mirror to slick on some lip balm. Two phones sounded like overkill to her, but it was sort of sweet how protective he was being. "Fine. Done. I promise to carry it with me at all times until this is over." Makeup done, she sidled around him and out into the bedroom. "Ready to go when you are."

Once they got to the station, a middle-aged female officer met them in the lobby. "Hi. I'm Lieutenant Dixon," she said, shaking both their hands. "First off, let me say to you, Neal, that I'm very sorry for your loss. I worked with your father several times on his cases and he was a good man."

"Thanks," Neal said, his expression stoic.

"And second," Lieutenant Dixon said, "thank you both for coming."

She led them down a hallway and into a small interrogation room with a table in the middle and windows on all sides. Lori and Neal took seats on one side of the table while the officer sat on the other. Dixon laid a pen and legal pad on the table in front of her and set a tiny digital recorder at the center of the table.

"Just in case I miss something," the officer said. "Don't always write as fast as I think I do."

"That's fine," Lori said. She went over everything that had happened so far for Lieutenant Dixon, from her initial theories about Gary being murdered that the police had brushed off, to the subsequent death threat note, to the days leading up to the fire.

The whole time, Lieutenant Dixon wrote on her legal pad, her scowl darkening more and more as the story continued. Finally, she put down her pen and looked at Lori, anger flashing in her dark eyes. "Well, I'm going to be honest here. I'm pissed off. I'm pissed that my own department didn't take your suspicions seriously, Ms. Hart. Because maybe if they had, we could have avoided all this."

"Do you have any leads on who might have set the blaze last night?" Neal asked, sitting back and crossing his arms. His leg nudged into the side of Lori's under the table, giving her a weird sense of security. Knowing he was there beside her made her feel stronger, which was odd for a woman who was used to standing on her own.

Lieutenant Dixon sighed and pushed her pad aside to clasp her hands on the table. "Well, we're not supposed to comment on active investigations, Mr. Ward."

"That asshole tried to kill her last night," Neal ground out, each word sharp as a razor blade. "I think we deserve to know what's going on so we can keep her safe."

"I don't even know what he looks like," Lori said. "It could be anyone." She shuddered as memories from the fire swamped her head. The panic, the terror, the choking finality that those could have been the last moments of her life and she still had so much she wanted to do, to experience, to be… Lori hugged her arms around her middle and squeezed. "I don't like feeling so vulnerable. What if he tries to come at me again?"

What if this time he succeeds?

She didn't say the words out loud, but apparently she didn't have to, if the way Neal's leg pressed tighter to hers and the fierce flash of protectiveness in his hazel eyes was any indication.

Lieutenant Dixon seemed to take that in a moment before giving a curt nod. She leaned in closer and lowered her voice. "You didn't hear this from me, okay? And if I find out either of you went after this man on your own, I will throw your ass in jail so fast you won't know what hit you. Yeah?"

Lori and Neal both nodded, leaning across the table too to meet Dixon halfway.

The officer took a deep breath and said, "Here's what we know so far. The fire was started with dry cleaning chemicals. And security footage from the alley shows that the man that Mr. Ward saw around the time the fire began was Curtis Hill."

"Curtis? The dry cleaner on the first floor?" Lori frowned. She knew the guy, had interacted with him regularly. He'd seemed nice enough, if a bit bland and boring. But apparently, there were sides to him that she had never imagined. He had tried to kill her. And if he'd done that, then there was a possibility he might have killed Gary too. The nebulous theories in her head suddenly coalesced into something far more real and terrifying.

Neal, who'd had less interaction with Curtis and was far less affected by the news, took charge. "Where is he now?" he asked. "Is he in police custody?"

"Not yet," Lieutenant Dixon said. "We're looking for him, but he's currently on the run."

Well, shit.

They finished up with the police and headed back out to the car, Neal watching her like she might crumble at the slightest breeze. "Are you okay?" he asked at last.

"I'm fine," she said, too fast, not looking at him.

Neal gave her some side eye, then must have decided to let that go for now, because he switched topics completely as they pulled out of the station parking lot. "So. Since the cops are handling searching for Curtis Hill, I say we should focus on trying to figure out how and why he murdered my dad."

She took a deep breath, straightened in her seat, and did her best to act professional. Even though it would have been really nice to crawl over into his lap and maybe work out her tension and anxiety in another way.

Stop it.

Lori cleared her throat, her voice still emerging rougher than she would have liked. "Agreed. What's our next step?"

"I think we need fresh eyes on this," he said, signaling before making a left turn onto a side street. "Let's go talk to my brothers."

"Okay." She was used to talking to clients. Used to questioning people, and also breaking hard news to them when her investigation turned up something she knew they wouldn't want to hear. But for some reason, once they got to Gary's house and were standing before

Neal's brothers to tell them the truth—that their father might have been murdered—she got tongue-tied. "I mean, it's just a theory I've been working on," she said, tripping over her words. "We still don't know for sure, but—"

"We think Dad was murdered," Neal cut in bluntly.

"What?" Ryan's affable smile morphed into shock, then upset. "What the hell, bro?"

"Fuck," Lance said, clearly pissed off. "This is the real reason you decided to stay in town, right? Why the fuck didn't you tell us this sooner?"

She went from feeling tongue-tied to feeling completely out of place, which wasn't any better. "Uh, maybe I should step outside for a minute."

"No. Stay here," Neal growled, holding his ground as he glared at his brothers.

When they all seemed more interested in angry stares than in talking things out, she decided it was time for her to step forward. "Look, I understand you all are hurt and you have every right to be upset. But right now our top priority needs to be catching Gary's murderer."

With that, the anger in the room dissipated enough that they could gather together again in the center without killing each other. Lori took a seat in an armchair, while the guys took the huge, oversized sofa.

It didn't take long for them to run through everything they'd done for the investigation so far. Neal sat forward, forearms resting on his thighs, and stared at his hands dangling between his knees. "I'll send over copies of what we have to you guys by tomorrow morning."

"Good." Lance rested his elbow on the opposite arm of the sofa, frowning. "We'll take a look."

"Yep." Ryan, stuck in the middle, scrubbed a hand over his face. "Maybe we'll find something you guys missed."

With that, Neal stood and headed for the door. Lori followed, only to be stopped by Lance at the threshold.

"Hey," Lance said, catching her arm. "Uh, thanks. For everything you've done so far." He looked a bit sheepish. "And for taking control earlier when we were posturing. You're good at running the show."

"Thanks." She grinned despite the situation. "I've had a lot of practice."

"I know." He exhaled slowly and hung his head. "And I'm sorry that we have to sell off the agency. We'll do everything we can to make sure you land on your feet."

"S-sell the agency?" she stammered. Sure, she'd known that the brothers would inherit the company's assets—the lease that was in their father's name, the insurance policy, the money in the business account, and the value of any current contracts—but she'd assumed they'd let her keep things running, maybe buy them out down the road when she was able to bring in enough contracts under her own steam. Selling…she hadn't had any idea.

"Yeah," Lance confirmed. "Harper Lewis Agency made us a great offer, just because Dad's business is older and has better name recognition." He cursed under his breath, then met her gaze. "Sorry. I guess what I'm trying to say is that we'll do everything we can to convince Harper Lewis to take you on after they buy us out, okay?"

Stunned, Lori whispered, "Okay. Thanks."

She stood on the porch after Lance closed the door, staring at nothing and wondering what the hell had just happened, while her life seemed to be falling down around her.

14

———————

By the time they got home that night, Neal was beat. Between the interview with the police and then the showdown with his brothers, all Neal wanted was a good meal, good company, good sex with Lori, and a good night's sleep. Not necessarily in that order.

Unfortunately, she didn't seem to be on the same page. After he fixed a quick dinner, they settled in on the couch to watch TV. Neal tried to hold her and kiss her, but she blew him off, claiming she was tired.

When he let himself feel the heaviness in his body, he had to admit that she had a point. After all, three out of four wasn't bad. Neal yawned and stretched before pushing to his feet. "Yeah, I'm exhausted too. Why don't we just go to bed early tonight?"

She shook her head and continued to stare at the screen, her toe tapping against the hardwood floor, and for the first time, it occurred to Neal that she might be upset with him. Her words confirmed it. "When were you going to tell me?"

He frowned, confused. "Tell you what?"

"That you and your brothers were selling the agency."

Oh shit.

He'd wondered back at his dad's house what Lance was talking to her about on the porch. And now he knew. Fuck. He tried to play it off. "I, uh, thought you knew already. I mean it's pretty clear none of us wanted to take over running it. If we'd had any interest at all in working at a PI agency we would've spent time with Dad, learning the ropes, getting licensed and all that. Not to mention, we've all got our lives waiting for us elsewhere—Lance back in DC with his job at the Pentagon, me in Cleveland, Ryan back with his team, once his leave is up."

"Right. I see." From the way she clicked off the TV and stood to face him, her expression mulish, Neal knew that what she saw was straight through his bullshit. "I thought that since we'd been working so well together on your dad's case, and since you don't really have anything tying you to Cleveland, that maybe you'd reconsidered staying and working at the agency."

"What?" He cringed. "No. I'd never work there, not at any PI agency. I saw what it did to my dad. How it took up his whole life, and destroyed our family in the process. Why the hell would I want to work there?"

"It wasn't the work that destroyed your family," Lori said, arms crossed, and gaze narrowed. "It was how your father handled it. He *chose* to bury himself in work. It doesn't have to be that way."

No, that couldn't be true. She just didn't understand. She didn't know what his childhood had been like, the way work was always the reason for why his father was never around.

"I don't want to talk about this right now," he said, wishing like hell they could go back to that morning and start the whole fucking day over again. Do it right this time, but just like his fucked-up childhood, it was too late to change things now.

"You never want to talk about anything, Neal. That's your problem." Lori stormed off down the hall, slamming her bedroom door with a resounding *thwack* that was the perfect ending to Neal's shitty evening.

Later, as he tossed and turned in his bed in the guest room, Neal kept going over in his head how it would all go from here. Last night, he'd wondered if Lori would come with him to Cleveland, start a new life there with him—and that was still what he wanted. Yes, things had gotten fucked tonight, thanks to Lance dropping a bombshell that Neal should have said something to her about days ago. But perhaps he could still salvage things. Maybe the agency closing didn't have to be an end, but a beginning.

They could even move somewhere new together. She was right that he wasn't attached to Cleveland. He was willing to take her wherever she wanted to go. Someplace with no PI agencies where they could leave all their emotional baggage behind. Between his disability pay from the navy and the money he'd saved over the years while serving, he could afford to take some time off, cover their expenses while they both got settled somewhere new.

He sighed and closed his eyes, but Lori's hurt, angry face kept popping up in his head, keeping him from sleep. Finally he sat up and stared at the shadows across the dark room. Maybe it was nuts, crazy, asking her about this now. They barely knew each other and had only slept together once. He should probably slow down.

But the thing was, there was something different about Lori. Different than anything he'd ever felt for any woman before. And frankly, he wasn't ready to give up and walk away from her just yet.

Neal was just about to lie down and try to sleep again when the sound of a door creaking open echoed from the hallway. Soon, footsteps followed, and his door opened on Lori in her PJs, looking as miserable as he felt. He held out a hand to her and she crawled into bed with him, snuggling into his side, all soft and warm and wonderful.

"I'm still mad at you, you know," she whispered against the side of his neck where her face was tucked. Her warm breath made him shiver and pull the covers tighter around them. "But I sleep better when you're here."

He made a sound of agreement low in his throat, taking it as a good sign, her being there, as they fell asleep in each other's arms.

The next morning, they were both up early, Neal making breakfast while Lori got dressed. She wasn't sure how guys did it, getting ready in like five minutes. She was fast, and didn't do a lot of complicated stuff with her hair or makeup or anything, but still. It took her at least half an hour.

Taking her time had its benefits, though, since by the time she got to the kitchen, the coffee and the food were done. She set the table and fixed herself a cup of joe, stopping behind Neal to kiss the back of his neck, smiling when he shuddered. Man, she loved making such a big tough guy melt like ice cream in her hands. "Hey," she said, as she carried the plates of scrambled eggs and bacon and toast he'd just dished up for them to her kitchen table. "I'm sorry about overreacting last night. I get that it makes sense for you guys to sell the agency." She took her seat and waited for Neal to join her at the table, pouring them each a glass of OJ. "You never promised me you were sticking around, and you don't owe me anything."

Her chest ached and she resisted the urge to rub the sore spot over her heart, picking up her fork and digging into her food instead.

"You know," she said, swallowing a bite of eggs, "I think I'm still upset about finding out Curtis tried to kill me. I trusted that weaselly little fucker and now I feel like I can't trust anyone anymore. Is that weird?"

"No." Neal frowned down at his plate, pushing his eggs around without eating any. He took a deep breath then looked up at her. "You could move to Cleveland with me," he said in a rush, the words tumbling over themselves. "Start over fresh."

"Oh." She blinked at him, a strip of bacon halfway to her mouth. That was…unexpected. And totally not feasible. Lori set the bacon down and wiped her hands. "What about my family? I can't leave them behind. And Lance mentioned something about putting in a good word for me at the agency that's buying your dad's place out. I mean, I'd rather keep working at Ward Investigation, but a steady job with an established firm is better than nothing."

"If you moved in with me, you wouldn't have to work at all—not right away," he muttered, dark brows knit as he stared at his plate again. "You could find something else to do that makes you happy."

"But I like working, Neal. I like what I do." She inhaled deeply, the indefinable ball of hurt swelling inside her like a balloon, squashing her appetite. "Look, I know that you don't like PI work and you don't want to run the agency, but it's important to me, okay? And honestly, the fact that you think I could just walk away and leave it all behind without even looking back makes me feel like you see zero value in something that I've poured my heart and soul into for the last three years."

"I…" he started, then stopped. Neal sighed, then tried again. "I just thought it could be a new beginning, for both of us. I want to see what the future could hold for us."

"I do too," she said, sitting back, wondering how such a lovely morning could turn sour so quickly. "I want to see what our future holds, Neal. But what if you can't get over this whole aversion to my career field, huh? I'm a PI, Neal. It's what I am. It's what I do. If you want me, that comes with the package."

The abrupt end to their conversation didn't bode well for the rest of the day either. They spent the rest of the morning and afternoon at the burned-out office, dodging insurance investigators while trying to pack up any files and personal effects that weren't completely destroyed.

Neal was quiet, filling up box after box with his dad's old stuff, not really saying much of anything, at least until he came across a photo. Lori moved in beside him to see a charred picture of him and Gary at Neal's high school graduation. She smiled. "Your dad had photos of all of you everywhere he could stick them on his desk. He was so proud of all of you."

He grunted and shoved it in the box with the rest of the stuff. "Makes it easier for me, shutting this place down." So much for any lingering hope that she might be able to convince him to keep the place open to honor his father's name.

After what felt like a small eternity in the fresh hell that the office had become, they went back to her house. Neal offered to make them dinner, but Lori wasn't hungry. Still too much stress and hurt churning inside her, so she opted out and settled onto the sofa with her laptop to do a last-minute background check for a regular client at the agency. The emergency request had come in via email earlier that day.

"There's really no point," Neal said from the kitchen where he was frying something in a pan. "Since we're shutting the agency down anyway. Might as well refer them on to the new place and be done with it."

Irritated, she rolled her eyes, then stared at her screen. He really needed to get off it. Just because he didn't like her choices, didn't mean he got to live in denial about them. "I'm keeping my options open and maintaining relationships," she replied, fingers flying across her keyboard. "Besides, I still need a paycheck. Have to keep the money coming in somehow."

At least this time, he didn't reply that he'd provide for her—that she could live like a princess in a castle and not have any work, or do anything that truly interested her. He'd learned enough not to make that argument. Now when would he learn to actually accept her for who she was?

15

---

eal sat at the kitchen table at his dad's house a few days later. Since the argument the other night—and since the office was now a burned-out pit unsuitable for working—Lori had suggested shifting their operations to Gary's place so that his brothers would be on hand to help. Since the fight, things between them hadn't been great. So, the space and extra people around was good.

Still, Neal wasn't a man who gave up easily, and he refused to throw in the towel on their relationship. Not yet. There had to be a way to fix things, to compromise. He just hadn't found it yet.

"Shit!" Ryan called from the living room, followed by the sound of his laptop closing. He swiveled in his desk chair to face Neal, scowling at him over the breakfast bar. "I've been scouring the Internet for hours and there's no liquid poisons I can find that would mimic a heart attack. At least, not anything that you could hide in coffee without the drinker noticing before they got a fatal dose." He gave a frustrated sigh and scrubbed a hand over his face. "Definitely nothing Curtis Hill could've gotten his hands on, anyway."

"Well," Lori said from her makeshift workstation in one of armchairs in the living room. "I managed to hack into Curtis's email account. Idiot used his company slogan and birth year for the password." She gave a rueful shake of her head. "When are people going to learn?"

"Find anything useful?" Neal asked.

"Nothing about poison or Gary," she said. "But from what I saw, our dry cleaner has a huge gambling problem."

"Really?" Neal got up and walked into the living room to stand behind Lori's chair and peer down at her screen. Lance and Ryan came over too. She brought up several emails to show them. "Looks like he used a couple of different online betting sites and lost a lot. He owed big-time debts to these places."

"Hmm." Lance leaned in closer, squinting at the screen. "I've heard of this site. I know someone who works there." He straightened and pulled out his phone. "Let me give him a call and see if he knows anything that might help us."

Lance walked down the hall for some privacy while Ryan headed into the kitchen for a drink.

Neal lingered behind, unable to make himself leave her side just yet. It was completely stupid, but damn if he didn't miss Lori. It made no sense. They spent almost all of their time together still—including their nights in her bed. They'd even had sex, though it wasn't quite the same as before the fight. Then it had felt sweet and slow and tender. Now, it felt more like a way to burn off their mutual frustration with their situation. The biggest change, though, was that they didn't really talk to each other. Not about personal stuff anyway, and that bothered him as much as anything else. He inhaled deeply, the scent of her shampoo making his chest ache with yearning and…

Dammit. Enough.

He turned away and closed his eyes, stalking back into the kitchen.

They'd hit a rough patch. Most couples did. They'd work through it eventually, right?

Neal flopped back down in his chair and scrolled through his computer screen without really seeing it. All he could picture was Lori, before the fight. Her laughing, her holding him, her smiling up at him all sleepy and sated after they'd made love.

It was enough to drive him nuts.

Luckily, Lance walked in and distracted him from his breakdown.

"Well, I just talked to the guy from the gambling site and I think we're on to something here with Curtis." He took the seat across the table from Neal while Ryan and Lori came in and joined them. "According to my friend, Curtis did owe his bookie a lot of money. Like in the seven-figures kind of debt. At least until the mob paid it all off for him."

"Fuck." The last thing Neal wanted to deal with right now was the mob. But then, what he wanted these days didn't seem to be fate's top priority.

"And from what my friend told me, I don't think the website he works for was the only one Curtis was in debt to."

"Oh boy." Ryan sat back, clasping his water bottle on the table. "So, why would the mob pay off all that debt for him?"

"That's a good question." Lori opened her laptop and clicked a few buttons, then looked at them over the top of her screen. "From what I can see here, it looks like at least four of the online gambling sites Curtis uses started taking bets from him again the last few weeks, so he must've been paid up with them too."

"That's our motive, then," Neal said, leaning back in his chair and sighing. "Curtis must be in the mob's pocket. With that kind of money on the line, they could easily have pressured him into doing something for them."

"You think Dad had something on the mob?" Ryan asked, frowning.

"Could've been a case he was working," Lance said, shrugging, then looked at Lori. "Were there any cases our dad was investigating involving organized crime? If so, maybe they had him killed to keep him quiet."

"Or maybe they had Curtis do it for them," Neal said. "Maybe that was what he had to do in exchange for them paying off his debt."

"Shit." Ryan shook his head and stood. "I'm going to call Lieutenant Dixon and let her know what we found out about the mob connection."

As Ryan left the room, Neal said, "Now we just have to figure out how Dad was killed."

Lance's phone buzzed and he got up as well. "I need to take this. Excuse me."

Lori closed her laptop and gave Neal a serious look. "Are you doing okay?"

He frowned. "Yeah. Why wouldn't I be?"

"I don't know." She shrugged. "I'm just thinking that it can't be easy for you to spend so much time here in your dad's house."

"It's fine." He stood to grab a water from the fridge. Offered Lori one too, but she declined. As he twisted off the lid and took a long drink, Neal was surprised to find that it was true. He was surprisingly okay with being here, in his dad's house, the house where Neal had grown up, with all the old memories clustered around him. In fact, working with his brothers and Lori these past few days had been kind of great, actually. It had been a long time since he'd spent this much time with his family, and he'd missed it. He knew his brothers were as dedicated to their duty as SEALs as he had been, but the fact that all three of them had been in service had meant that they were rarely able to all get together at once—and never for so many days in a row.

His heart sank as he realized that that kind of family time was exactly what he was asking Lori to give up if she moved to Cleveland with him. Time with her mother and her sister. Time with her niece Hope. It wasn't a fair thing to ask. He saw that now.

With a sigh, he set his water aside, then bent and kissed Lori quickly on the mouth before heading toward the living room himself.

"I need to make a call too," he said, walking to the front door. "I'll be out on the porch if you need me."

The air was brisk today, but it felt good. Bracing. Bold. Just like he needed to be if he was going to fix the mess he'd created between him and Lori. He pulled out his cell and dialed the number for an old friend who owned a local manufacturing company. It wasn't exactly PI work, but if he could get her a good job in manufacturing, maybe doing their safety inspections and employee background checks, that would kind of be PI adjacent, right? And yeah, she'd need additional training for the OSHA stuff and all, but Lori was smart. She'd pick it right up.

Of course, he'd need a job too. He still planned to freelance security service, but it might take a while to build up a clientele like he'd done in Cleveland. Still, if he was going to ask her to leave the PI world she loved, then he needed to sacrifice too by moving back to Detroit. He wanted to make sure he had good opportunities lined up for them both before he talked to her about it again. Maybe his friend might have something for him too, to see him through until Neal's business was up and running again.

16

Later that night, they were back at her house and Lori was in the shower. It was one of the few places where she had the peace and quiet to think these days, and thinking was exactly what she was doing. Mainly about how she might be able to scrape together enough money to put in an offer on the agency.

She'd done some online research about it earlier and had found some good resources. She'd also come to the conclusion that she didn't want to work for another agency in town. They'd worked too hard to maintain Ward Investigation as the top agency in Detroit to just sell it off to the highest bidder. It felt like a betrayal.

No. She wanted to keep the agency she'd put her heart and soul into the past three years. Keep it and build it into something even greater. Modesty aside, Lori thought she'd be pretty damned good at it.

Buying it out made the most sense. That way, there was no chance Neal would be her boss or her coworker, and he could go back to the security work he liked and stay out of the agency that he hated.

Between her savings from her last job, a contribution from her parents, and a loan from the bank, Lori thought she could probably scrape together enough for an offer that was on the low side, but at least not laughable.

She was still working through the numbers in her head as she got out of the shower, dried off, and changed into her PJs. Heading down the hall to the kitchen, Lori stopped short at the sight of Neal on the floor, doing what looked like extremely angry push-ups.

"Uh, what are you doing?"

He scowled at the floor, the muscles in his arms bulging with effort. "What's it look like I'm doing?"

"Pissed-off push-ups?"

"Got it in one." He halted mid-push-up and winked at her.

She stepped over him to grab a water from the fridge. "My real question is, why are you doing pissed-off push-ups in my kitchen? What's wrong?"

He grunted through a few more reps, then slumped back against the cabinets, wiping his sweaty face with a dish towel which he then slung over his shoulder. Neal frowned down at his hands in his lap. He looked like a lost puppy, sad and defeated, and part of her wanted nothing more than to get down on the floor with him and hold him until his smile returned. But the other part of her knew that he had a bunch of things to work through here emotionally, and distracting him from them wouldn't help anything. So she stayed where she was across the room and took a sip of her water, giving him time and space to open up to her when he was ready.

"I don't know what's wrong exactly," he said, toying with the end of the towel. "I just keep thinking about the last voicemail message I got from my dad." He sighed, his dark brows drawing together. "I didn't even listen to it. Just deleted it right away." Neal looked up at her, his hazel eyes bright with pain. "What if it was something important, Lori? What if it was something that could've saved his life or helped us with the case now?"

Dammit. So much for keeping her distance.

She set her water aside and walked over to him, holding out her hand to help him up, even though he was twice her size. Instead of letting him go once he was on his feet, however, she pulled him into a hug, wrapping her whole body around him to make him feel safe and loved, the same way she did for Hope when she was upset. "Listen, you can't blame yourself for that, okay? You didn't know what was going to happen." She pulled back slightly as an idea occurred to her. "Maybe if you contact your carrier, they can recover the message. I've had them do that for me on cases. If you want, I can contact them for you tomorrow."

Neal stared down at her a second, then bent and kissed her, soft and sweet. Her heart melted into a puddle near her toes. "Thank you."

Lori smiled, wondering when it had gotten so hot in there. "You're welcome."

She started to step away, but Neal stopped her. In an instant, he was kissing her again and things went from sweet to steamy in about two seconds flat. She couldn't seem to get enough of him. From the way Neal was kissing and nuzzling and stroking her, his hands seeming to be everywhere on her at once, he apparently felt the same way. He leaned his hips back against the counter, spreading his legs to draw her between them. His hard cock pressed against her lower belly, leaving her in no doubt that he wanted her every bit as much as she wanted him. But there were still things she needed to do, numbers to crunch. With her last shred of sanity, Lori forced herself to pull back, her hands on his bare chest over his thundering heart. "I should, uh, get back to work. Still have things to do."

"Or…" Neal said, sliding his hands down her sides to her waist, then picked her up and spun her around to set her on the counter, reversing their positions. He stepped between her spread legs, running his hands up her inner thighs, his thumbs skimming the sensitive line where her legs joined her torso through her thin cotton PJs, making her shiver. "You could leave that work until later and stay here and do *me*."

In the end, that was no decision at all.

She dug her fingers into his short dark hair and pulled him to her for a hot, open-mouthed kiss, grinding the heat between her legs against his rock-hard abs. Oh yeah. This was going to be good. So, so good.

Neal quickly unbuttoned her PJ top and took it off her, lavishing his attention on her breasts while she moaned and gasped and held him close, telling him what she wanted, needed, him to do to her. She'd never been all that vocal during sex before, but with Neal it was different. With Neal, everything was different.

Then his fingers traced her skin above the waistband of her pants, and Lori trembled against him. "Please…" she begged.

"Please what, darlin'?" he asked, nuzzling the spot just below her earlobe that drove her wild with lust.

"Please touch me."

He leaned back, flashing her a wicked smile. "Oh, darlin'. I'm going to touch you. I'm going to taste you. I'm going to make you scream as you come for me."

She damned near dissolved into a puddle of need right there on the counter. Her breath caught as he made good on his promise, kneeling before her, their height difference putting him in a perfect position between her legs. Slowly, so slowly, he pulled off her PJ pants, his eyes locked with hers the whole time. His pupils were blown wide with lust, nearly eclipsing the hazel. Knowing how much he wanted her drove her own desire higher. Then he leaned in and kissed her slick folds through her panties, teasing her with his tongue and lips until she thought she might lose her mind from lust. She held him there, begging him for more.

Finally, he put her out of her misery and removed her panties too, tossing them over his shoulder to join the growing pile of her clothes on the floor. Lori sat naked on the edge of her counter, the cold granite beneath her butt a sharp contrast to the sizzling heat inside her. Then Neal put his mouth on her again, lavishing attention on her with his lips and fingers and tongue as he brought her to one climax after another, until her mind was fuzzy with pleasure and her bones felt like mush. Only then did he pick her up and carry her to the bedroom, where he put her in the middle of her bed before stripping himself, putting on a condom, then sliding over her, sliding into her, taking her back to the peak of climax again all too soon. It was good. It was so, so good.

Neal shifted his angle of penetration until he was hitting inside of her just right, sending her hurtling over the edge one last time before coming hard inside of her himself, her name on his lips and his breath hot on her neck.

Afterward, once he'd fallen asleep half sprawled on top of her, Lori stayed awake, gliding her fingers through his soft hair, whispering, "I'm not giving up on us. I'm not ready to give up on us."

She'd buy the agency. Help Neal relocate his business to Detroit and meet new clients in town. Or, if worse came to worst, he'd stay in Cleveland and she'd drive down there on the weekends to see him.

Either way, they'd figure it out.

A couple of evenings later, Lori walked into the kitchen, smiling. "I just got an email from your cell company. They were able to recover your dad's last voicemail message."

Neal glanced back at her over his shoulder from where he was cooking them dinner at the stove, then shut off the burner. "Yeah? That's great. Let's hear it."

They took seats at the table next to each other and she put her phone on speaker, then hit the link for the recording before setting the phone on the table. Within seconds, Gary's voice echoed through the kitchen and Lori's heart ached. Man, she missed the guy.

"Neal, son," Gary said. "I'm sorry to bother you. I know you're busy with your own clients, but I've got a case I could really use your help on." Neal and Lori locked eyes as the message continued. "Anyway, this one's getting dangerous. I think someone powerful here in Detroit is poisoning people and making the deaths look like heart attacks." It felt like the earth rocked beneath Lori's feet and she grasped Neal's hand without thinking. From the way the blood had drained from his tanned face, he felt similarly. "Look, son. I know we've had our problems and we don't always see eye to eye." Gary chuckled. "Okay. We never see eye to eye these days—we haven't for a long, long time. But like I said, Neal, I could really use your help here. I think this one might be too big for me, and I sure could use someone who knows how to stand tall in the line of fire, and who I could trust to watch my back." The sound of Detroit traffic echoed through the phone line as Gary paused. Then he finished with, "Also, if anything happens to me, son, can you please look out for Lori? She's a good kid, even if she's too curious for her own good."

The message ended there.

Lori blinked hard against the sting of tears in her eyes, her chest tight.

Neal didn't move, didn't say a word for a long moment. Just stared at her phone like he wanted to burn a hole through it. Then he cursed and stood, pulling away from her, scrubbing his hands through his hair. "Fuck. I feel awful now."

"Hey," she said, doing her best to comfort him. "It's okay. You didn't know."

"But I should have, dammit." He turned to face her, his expression stricken. "He hardly ever called me. The fact he did then should've told me it was important." He hung his head. "Maybe if I'd listened to that message then, my dad would still be alive."

Lori got up from the table and walked over to him, cupping his cheeks. "Listen to me. We talked about this. Gary's death was not your fault. He knew the risks he was taking. It's part of the job and he was willing to do it. Stop blaming yourself for this. It's not helping anyone, least of all you, okay?"

He blinked at her a moment and Lori worried that he was going to pull away again, shut down on her. But this time he didn't. Neal took a deep breath, then another, before his broad shoulders finally slumped. Lori's hands slid down to his chest. "Maybe you're right. Maybe if Dad had made different choices with his life, left the PI industry years ago and chosen to put his family first, he'd still be alive." He shook his head and stared up at the ceiling for what felt like a small eternity before meeting her gaze. "What if you keep working as a PI and something bad like that happens to you, huh?" He covered her hand on his chest with his, squeezing them tight. "I couldn't stand it if you got caught up in some dangerous mess like Dad did and you got killed, Lori."

She frowned, stepping back and tugging her hands free. The conversation had taken a turn she hadn't expected. "That's not fair, Neal.

Being a PI is no more dangerous than what you do in your security business. No different than what your brothers do in the military. All of those jobs come with risk. Hell, life is risky, Neal." She held her hands up, exasperated. "I could walk out the door and get hit by a bus right now. You almost died yourself in a war zone when that IED blew up beneath the car you were driving." Lori shook her head and crossed her arms. "I don't understand why being a private investigator is the one thing you can't seem to get past, Neal."

A small muscle ticked near his jaw and his eyes flashed with pain and regret. His words were jagged with tension. "Because private investigators work alone, Lori. Without a team. When I was in the SEALs, like my brothers are now, I knew someone always had my back. You've got no one. You're out there on your own. That's what's different."

Hurt and frustrated, she couldn't let that drop. "Well, then. Maybe you should stay in Detroit and be part of my team when this is over."

Neal opened his mouth, closed it, then opened it again before his walls fell back into place. His expression went stoic once more and Lori knew she'd lost him. Again.

"I don't want to talk about this," he said, pushing away from the counter and stalking out into the living room. "I need to call Lance and Ryan and let them know about that message. Tell them we might have a new lead in the case." He glanced back at her as if nothing had happened just now, like he hadn't just stabbed her in the heart with his old fears and new prejudices about a job she loved. She swallowed hard and forced herself to stand there, instead of running back to her bedroom and locking herself away for a good long cry. Neal pulled on his jacket and headed for the door, still talking about the case instead of addressing the elephant in the room between them. "If Dad was killed the same way as the people he was investigating, then we're looking for poisons that mimic heart attacks that would be available to the mob, and not just Curtis." He opened the door, then stopped on the threshold. "If we can find the men whose deaths Dad was investigating, and how they died, then maybe we can work out how Dad was killed too."

It was the break they'd been hoping for with the case. She just wished it hadn't come along with a broken heart for her.

17

The next morning, they were back at his dad's place.

Neal and Lori had worked with his brothers for hours, trying to figure out which cases their dad had worked on that might have anything to do with heart attacks. Unfortunately, Neal had spent days going through his father's most recent files, and couldn't remember anything that seemed connected to that. And it wasn't like they could do much to check the files again, considering how much damage the contents of the filing cabinets had taken in the fire.

"Maybe he hid them outside the office, and that's why you didn't find anything promising when you were going through those files the first time?" Ryan suggested. "We could search the house again. I could use a break from sitting anyway. My ass has been numb for a while."

"Agreed," Lori said, standing and stretching. "Uh, before we all separate to do that, though, there's something I wanted to talk to all of you about, together."

"About the case?" Lance asked, frowning.

"No. Non-case related." Lori sounded a bit nervous, and Neal's instincts went on high alert. He didn't like the sound of this already. "It won't take long."

"Okay," Ryan said, settling back down in his chair beside Lance.

Neal remained on his feet, too restless to sit.

"So," Lori said, smiling. "I have a business proposal for you."

Hell. No.

"I want to buy your dad's agency." Her gaze flicked to Neal before returning to Lance and Ryan. "Listen, I know this might come as a shock to you and you've already had at least one solid offer already, but seriously. You won't find anyone who's more passionate about the business than me, or who knows your dad's company and his clients better."

"Uh, wow. Okay." Ryan said, giving Lance some side eye. "I guess we need to talk about this, then."

"We were pretty close to closing the deal with Harper Lewis, but I suppose we could consider another offer," Lance said, "since nothing's been finalized yet."

"No." Neal stepped forward, putting himself between his brothers and Lori.

"Why not?" Lori said, staring up at him defiantly. "I'm making a legitimate offer here."

Shit.

He needed to stay cool. Had to handle this the right way, to avoid an epic disaster like the last time they'd discussed this.

"Can I, uh." He cleared his throat and tried again. "Can I talk to you in private for a minute?"

Lori gave him a flat look, then shook her head. "Fine. Whatever."

They went down the hall into one of the guest rooms and Neal closed the door behind them for some privacy. He took a deep breath and launched into his spiel. He'd been hoping to do this later, when they were back home at her house and relaxed, but she'd forced his hand just now.

"So, I've been talking to a buddy of mine who owns a big private security firm. They're opening a new office here in Detroit. I've worked with them before with clients in Cleveland and they're really good. Anyway, he's looking for someone to help him market the company in this region and meet with potential new clients here before their grand opening. I told him about your background in marketing and showed him your LinkedIn profile and even vouched for you personally. He thinks you'd be a perfect fit."

Still nothing from Lori, so he kept on going, because what the hell else was he going to do at this point? He placed his hands on her arms, noting that she stayed stiff beneath his touch. Not good.

"Come on. Private security isn't that different from PI work. You'll still be helping people, just from the marketing side. Not to mention, you'll be better paid, have more regular hours, and in this new position, you'd be safe behind a desk instead of out in the field." He forced a smile. "I'm even willing to move back here to my hometown for you. If you're willing to stop being a PI."

No response. Oh boy. He was fucking this up even worse than before. He stepped back and raked a hand through his hair. "Please, Lori. I want to build a life with you, I do. But I've already seen this work destroy one family. I won't let it happen again."

Lori watched him, then exhaled slowly, her cheeks flushed and her eyes hard. "That's the most ridiculous thing I've ever heard."

"Well, that's the way it is," Neal countered. This was too important not to hold his ground. "It's either me, or your PI job. I care about you, Lori. A lot. But I can't go back to the same situation that ruined my home and my family."

"So that's it, then?" She held up her hands, her expression disbelieving. "You give me an ultimatum and I just have to take it or leave it? Please don't do this to me, Neal."

He stood firm, because that was what he'd been trained to do. That was what he'd learned to do after years of being forced to grow up too fast, thanks to his dad's workaholic neglect.

They stared at each other for a long, difficult second; then Lori turned away. "Fine. If that's the choice you're giving me, then I choose the job, Neal. I'm sorry. I guess we're breaking up. I love my work, but it's more than that. If you demand I give up something that important to me once, what's to stop you from doing it again, huh? If you think I'm working too much or what I want conflicts with your career, will you deliver another ultimatum? No." She sidled around him and walked to the door before turning back to him. "No. I refuse to let a man have that kind of control over me, over my career."

"I won't demand anything else about your career after this, Lori. I swear," he said, as everything he'd ever wanted was slipping away. "I promise you I won't. It's just this one thing." He gave a sad snort. "I even found you a better position to take its place. Don't you trust me?"

Lori blinked at him, tears in her eyes. "That's the problem, Neal. If this is your demand, then no. I don't trust you."

She walked out, leaving Neal behind feeling like his chest had been ripped open and his heart had been blown to pieces.

Eventually, he walked back out to the living room to find Lori packing up her computer and Ryan pulling on his jacket. Neal scowled. "What's going on?"

Ryan gave him a caught-in-the-middle look. "Uh, Lori asked me to take her home," he said, leaning in closer to Neal to whisper. "Don't worry, dude. I got this. I'll keep an eye on her until all of this is over. Won't let anything happen to her while I stay there."

This was sounding like a hell of a lot more than just giving her a ride. "Excuse me?" Neal looked from his brother to Lori, that chasm in his heart widening to Grand Canyon proportions. "He's staying at your house now?"

"I know it's not safe for me to be there by myself, and after what just happened between us, you can't stay there," Lori said, like it was obvious and he was an idiot. And sure, he felt like the biggest idiot on earth, but hearing that she thought so too made him feel about an inch tall. "And don't worry about helping me babysit tomorrow either. Ryan will do it. Since my mom has a doctor's appointment, we're watching Hope at Alison's place."

She walked out the front door, leaving Neal to stare after her. Loss hit him like a ballistic missile. Gone. Lori was gone. His childhood was gone. His dad was gone. Everything was gone.

All because of that goddamned PI agency.

"Sorry, dude," Ryan said, and then he left too, the sound of his car engine starting and pulling away the final note of Neal's shit-tastic symphony.

"You okay?" Lance asked from behind him.

No. Neal was not okay. He doubted he would be okay any time soon, if ever. He was tired. So fucking tired of losing things he cared about to a job he hated. He stormed across the living room and grabbed an empty box from the corner before charging up the stairs two at a time.

"Neal?" Lance called from the first floor. "What the hell are you doing?"

He rushed down the second-floor hall and into his old room, throwing everything he could grab into the box without looking at it as he yelled, "What I fucking told you to do days ago. Getting rid of this shit."

When his first box was full, he grabbed another, then another, filling them with all his old memories, all his old hurt, all his old pain. It helped, at least in the moment. A sort of white-noise buzz filled his head as he finished stripping his old room and moved on to the next room and the next, breathing hard and sweating a little. He didn't care. Working hard felt good. Felt cathartic. He was tired of carrying all this shit around. Time to let it go. Let it all go.

Sometime around the fourth room, he stopped and took a break, staring at the ghost images of the photos that used to be on the walls, marked by brighter, unfaded squares in the wallpaper. He stuck his hand into his jacket pocket—no wonder he was so hot, he hadn't even realized he was wearing the damned thing—to grab the tin of mints there, and found a post-it instead. Frowning, he pulled it out to find a note from Lori. She was always doing silly stuff like that for him. Leaving little flirty notes in places he didn't expect. This one was from that morning, actually. He'd forgotten he'd stuck it in there with everything else going on. She'd stuck it to his forehead while he'd been sleeping, telling him to join her in the shower when he woke up.

The spot in his chest where his heart had been seemed to collapse in on itself and he crumpled into a chair against the wall. He loved these notes. Loved the casual warmth of them. Loved the fact that she thought of him a lot, same as he did her. Loved that Lori cared about him. He cared about her, too. So much he ached with it.

He loved Lori.

The words were new, but the feeling wasn't. He just hadn't put a label on it until now.

Jesus. He loved Lori and now he'd lost her.

Neal hung his head and rubbed his eyes. He was so lost in his emotional shitstorm that he didn't even hear Lance come upstairs until his older brother was standing in the doorway, looking at him.

"I'm sorry about you and Lori," he said, leaning a shoulder against the doorframe. "What happened?"

After a deep breath, Neal told him. It was a relief, really, to get it all out there. "So, yeah, I fucked up."

Lance pushed off the doorframe and patted him on the shoulder as he passed. "Well, don't be too hard on yourself. Happens to the best of us. I wonder sometimes if it's genetic."

"Right." Neal gave a sad snort. "You fucked up pretty bad too, huh? With Ruth."

His older brother gave him a hard look, then shook his head and changed the subject fast. "What are you going to do about it?"

"Nothing. She doesn't want anything to do with me." Neal sighed and sat back, staring up at the ceiling. "I guess I'll just let it go, like every-thing else." His gut cramped. Letting Lori go was very nearly the last thing he wanted to do, but the one thing that topped that list was that he didn't want to hurt her again, and damn if he knew how to keep her without causing her more pain. "What else can I do?"

"You know," Lance said, walking over to the far wall and tracing his fingers around one of the empty spots where a photo used to be. If Neal remembered right, it was one of Lance and Ruth together, back when they'd been happy. This room had been his older brother's growing up. Lance sighed and let his hand drop to his side, his expres-sion thoughtful. "Just because something ends badly, doesn't mean it wasn't good. And it doesn't mean it's not worth holding onto and fighting for."

"Maybe, sometimes." He shrugged and let his head hang, so he was staring at the floor, the sticky note still clutched in his hand. "But I'm exhausted, from carrying all this baggage around inside of me, man. I don't want to hold on to all this old stuff. I want to make room for the new." *For Lori.*

Lance blinked at him a moment, then nodded and walked out of the room. "Okay then. Let's do it."

Neal followed him out into the hall, stopping near the box of stuff from his room. Sitting on top was his old stuffed bear, Mr. Moto. His dad had given him that. And yeah, it had been his favorite. Without thinking, he picked it up and stared into its one remaining dark glass eye, the pink stitched nose that was half gone now, rubbed away by many nights of holding the bear while he slept. An unexpected prickle stung his eyes and he blinked hard, scowling as his chest ached anew.

Just because something ends badly...it doesn't mean it's not worth holding onto and fighting for.

Maybe it would be okay to hold onto this much—just this much—while letting everything else go. He tucked the bear inside his jacket and stuffed the note back into his pocket before following Lance back downstairs.

18

Back at home, Lori wasn't doing too well herself.

At the time, it had felt good to stand up to Neal, to tell it like it was and exactly where he could shove his ultimatum. Because she was an independent, smart, savvy woman who didn't need the patriarchy telling her what she could and could not do.

It was good. It was fine.

Except she didn't feel fine now. She felt shitty.

Lori sank down onto the side of her bed and tucked her hands between her knees, glancing at the closed bedroom door before finally letting her tears fall. And once they started, they didn't stop. Great big, loud, wracking sobs. The kind of ugly crying that made people stop and stare if you were out in public. Total wailing and gnashing of teeth level sadness. Yep. Because Lori wasn't a person who did things by halves and she'd just lost the love of her life, so…

A quiet knock sounded on the door, followed by Ryan's somewhat sheepish voice. "Everything okay in there?"

No. Everything was most definitely not okay.

But Lori didn't want to say that to him. He was helping her out here, after all. Besides, he was Neal's brother and the last thing she wanted was for him to go back and tell Neal that she'd been a blubbering mess without him. Even if it was true, a girl had her pride, after all.

"Yes," she managed to call back a few seconds later, swiping her hands over her wet cheeks, then fumbling for a tissue from the box on the nightstand. "I'm good. Just, uh… doing a little cleaning."

Smooth, dumbass.

For a PI, who sometimes had to come up with effective aliases on the fly, lying wasn't her strong suit, obviously. She blew her nose, then added, "Dust allergies."

Thankfully, Ryan let it drop. Instead, there was a slight bump against the door; then he said, "I made you some hot chocolate. Always helps me when I've had a day from hell. I'll just leave it out here in the hall for you when you're done… cleaning."

"Thanks," she said, sniffling all over again. How sweet was that?

Dammit. She didn't want Ryan to be sweet to her, because it only reinforced to her what she'd lost with Neal. The chance to be with him, to be part of his family. And sure, she and her mom and Alison and Hope were close, but the more time she spent with the Ward brothers, the more they reminded her of their father, and how she and Gary worked together, compensating for each other's shortcomings. Neal and his brothers were strong where she was weak, and it had been wonderful to lean on that strength through this difficult time.

She'd thought she'd be able to do that for a lifetime with Neal.

Oh God. Neal.

Ryan's footsteps echoed back down the hall toward the living room, where he'd posted himself to guard her for the night. The Ward brothers were nothing if not dedicated to their self-appointed missions.

After wallowing in her sadness a little while longer, Lori took a shower and changed into her PJs before heading out of her room again. Hiding away from the world wasn't getting her anywhere, and she wasn't really one to cower anyway. Nope. She needed to face reality and figure out where to go from here, no matter how difficult it might be now.

That same determination had been what had gotten her through the whole mess with her ex, Jordan, when he'd tried to frame her for his embezzlement. It was what had driven her to get her PI license at night while working for Gary at the agency all day, because she'd finally found her true vocation, work that made her feel like she was doing what she was always meant to do in life. And it was what would get her through this break-up with Neal.

Because she loved him with all her heart, but true love shouldn't come with ultimatums.

She stopped to pick up her mug of hot chocolate from the corner where Ryan had left it by her door, then went out into the living room where he was sitting and clicking through channels on her TV.

"Mind if I join you?" she asked.

"Sure. Of course," he said, tossing the remote aside. "It's your house."

Lori smiled and curled up on the opposite end of the sofa from him, tucking her feet under her, then sipping her hot chocolate. It was good, with the little marshmallows she liked on top of it. She spotted an identical mug on the coffee table in front of Ryan.

"Thanks again for making this," she said, lifting her mug slightly. "I can't remember the last time I had it—I'm surprised you were even able to find it in my cabinets. My mom used to make it for us all the time in the winter when Alison and I were little, though."

He nodded, giving her a crooked grin. "Yeah. Same here. Though it was usually Neal who made it for me when I was upset." Her composure wobbled slightly, and Ryan's eyes widened. "Sorry. Didn't mean to poke a sore spot. Sorry." He held his hands up like he could ward off her tears. "Please don't cry."

For some reason, his panic struck Lori as funny and the humour staved off another sob session, thankfully. She sniffled and shook her head. "I think I'm done with that for a while. At least I'll try to be."

"Thanks." He settled back into his end of the sofa with his hot chocolate, looking relieved. "I mean, I can handle snipers and war zones just fine, but seeing a woman cry..." He shuddered. "Just gets me right in the feels, you know?"

Lori grinned. "That's sweet."

Ryan lifted a shoulder and swallowed a large gulp of hot chocolate. "Just being decent, right?"

"I suppose." She stared down into her mug as the TV droned on in the background. She didn't really feel like talking but didn't want to be rude. "So," she said, searching for a topic. "You're home on leave right now?"

If she hadn't been watching him, she wouldn't have noticed it—but he tensed just for a second. Less than a second, really, and then he relaxed again, making her wonder if she'd just imagined it. "Yeah. Bereavement leave. You know how it is."

"Sure," she said. "I mean, I've never lost a parent, so I don't really know how that feels, but I'm sure it's hard."

"Yeah, it is." He stared at the TV for a while and Lori stayed silent, both of them lost in their own thoughts, until Ryan looked over at her again. "Both your parents are around, then? I don't think I ever asked, but Neal did mention something about your mom."

She smiled. "Yes. My mom and stepdad are both alive and well. My mom's a travel agent and my stepdad owns a body shop here in town."

"Nice." Ryan muted the TV and shifted to face her on the sofa. "What about your bio dad? If it's not too personal for me to ask. If it is, then just tell me to fuck off. That's what my brothers do."

Lori smiled. "No, it's fine. My biological dad left my mom when I was ten. She found him cheating on her and he walked out on us for good. We lived in North Carolina then. The court gave him visitation rights, but he usually blew it off. And after we moved to Detroit, he didn't bother keeping in touch. I haven't seen or talked to him since."

"I'm sorry."

"It's fine. Wasn't like he was around all that much before the divorce anyway," she said. "He was always working."

"Hmm." Ryan nodded. "I can relate to that." He snorted. "I'm sure you know about that from Neal. He always took that really hard."

"But you didn't?" she asked, intrigued by how people living in the same household could view things differently.

He shrugged. "It was just the way it was. I guess I never spent much time wondering if it could be any different. Dad was Dad—he wasn't going to change. I could meet him where he was, or I could fight with him all the time, trying to get him where I wanted him to be. I mostly chose to meet him where he was."

"That's a tough lesson for a kid to learn," Lori pointed out.

"Turned out to be a tough lesson for adults to learn, too," he replied. "That's what happened with my mom."

Lori hid a wince. Gary hadn't talked much about his second wife—the only reason she knew he had one was because she'd done the math one time when he was talking about Ryan's birthday and had realized that Ryan had been born two years after Gary's first wife had died. A shamefaced Gary had admitted that she'd been a fling—but when they hadn't been careful enough with the birth control, he'd felt honor-bound to marry her and try to make things work. It hadn't gone well.

"Mom walked out when I was eight. Couldn't stand putting up with Dad's absentee father shit anymore. Not that she was one to talk—she wasn't all that interested in being there for me either, before or after walking out on Dad."

Without thinking, Lori reached across and placed her hand on his arm. "Now I'm sorry."

"No big deal. I mean, I was hurt when she left, don't get me wrong. But even then, I already knew she wasn't really someone who could be counted on. Not like my brothers. Neal and Lance were always there for me, you know? Neal especially, since Lance had graduated high school when I was seven and was off in the Navy, so most of the time after Mom left, it was just me and Neal at home. He really stepped up to take care of me. Cooked, cleaned, helped me with my homework. All the stuff a dad usually does, since ours was working all the time."

Her chest constricted again, both from the loss of Neal and from the reminder of everything Gary's sons had been through growing up. Hearing Ryan talk about it too really drove it home. It was hard to hear. She'd loved Gary. Looked up to him as both a mentor and a friend. Had wanted to pattern her life after his, at least professionally. But on the personal side, he didn't belong on the pedestal she'd built for him. Looking back, she could see that Gary had known that, too.

He hadn't been the type to talk much about his regrets, but she saw the way he was with Hope, heard the few things he'd say about how much he'd missed of his own boys' lives when they were that age. He'd been aware of his own flaws.

"So, what got you into PI work?" Ryan asked.

She told him about Gary hiring her three years ago, and working her way through night classes to get her license. "I just really enjoy the work."

"I can tell." He grinned. "What did you do before then?"

Lori toyed with the mug in her hands. She didn't talk about this much because it was too painful. But she was already raw from the break-up and things seemed so cozy and comfortable here with Ryan that she found herself opening up to him, telling him the whole story about Jordan. "Back then I was shocked and hurt and livid," she admitted as she talked about the aftermath. "Jordan had taken something that I'd loved and turned it against me, twisted it with his lies and his bullshit." She fiddled with the hem of her PJ top. "But looking back on it now, I'm almost grateful for the way things turned out. Gary helped me through. He got me out of that situation and gave me a job as his administrative assistant. It was less prestigious, and I had to take a cut in pay, but your dad was good to me and he never outright lied to me, even if he didn't always tell me the whole truth. And I ended up liking the work better anyway. Being an investigator is what I was always meant to do, and I might never have known that if Jordan hadn't been such a douchebag."

"Wow, that's… wow." He set his mug aside too. "Thanks for sharing that with me."

Lori smiled. "Thanks for listening. And for filling in for Neal on guard duty tonight."

"Of course." Ryan smiled, then got up to take their dirty cups to the kitchen. He stopped halfway there and looked back at her. "Don't give up on Neal so fast, though, huh? He's going through a lot right now and he didn't handle things the way he should have, but he's a good man. Give him a chance to work it out for himself and he'll get there, I promise."

She kept thinking about that, even after she went to bed. She was still hurt by Neal's inability to see how much her work meant to her and his crazy idea that she needed him to take care of her, as if she couldn't take care of herself. But on the other hand, he was also extremely kind and caring, putting others' safety and well-being ahead of his own. He'd done that with his SEAL team when he'd taken the brunt of that explosion himself to save the lives of others. He'd done that with Ryan growing up, acting as the responsible father figure for him and giving him a stable home. And he'd done that with Lori too, guarding her against asshole Curtis and saving her from the fire, being there for her after the funeral when she'd needed a shoulder to cry on.

God, she missed him. So much that it was hard to breathe sometimes.

She'd told him they were done, but maybe they weren't. Maybe she wasn't.

Lori fell asleep, still thinking about how in the world she might go about rebuilding things with Neal. Not the same as they were, but better.

19

The next morning, she and Ryan were up early and on their way to her mom's house to babysit Hope. She'd worn yoga pants and a comfortable top, knowing she'd be running around a lot after her niece. She adjusted the seatbelt across her chest, the burner phone stuck in her bra today because she had no pockets. The stupid thing kept poking her. She'd wanted to leave it at home, but she'd promised Neal she'd keep it on her at all times. And even though they were on the outs right now, she didn't want to break her word to him.

She did have her crossbody bag with her too, but it was small and already had her other phone in there plus her wallet and keys and lip gloss, so yeah. No room.

The radio was on, and Ryan was talking over it, going on about some soccer game that was happening at Lions stadium that weekend. She only half-listened, part of her mind on the Curtis Hill case and the other on the fact that she was going to need a hell of a lot more coffee to get through the day. Her sleep had been restless. She kept waking up and reaching for Neal across the bed, only to find nothing but a cold mattress.

Traffic was surprisingly sparse this morning, especially on the quiet, residential streets they were taking. They'd just paused at a stop sign before making a turn and Lori was fiddling with her phone, texting her mom to let her know they were almost there, when the accident happened.

At first, Lori wasn't sure what was going on. One second, Ryan was talking and the radio was playing Bon Jovi and the sun was shining in the windows, then boom. Glass was flying everywhere and they were tumbling, tumbling, tumbling across the road and into a ditch. Never one to be good with spinning anyway, Lori's stomach went sour even as her mind scrambled to figure out what the fuck was happening. The accident itself only took seconds, but inside their car, it felt as though time had slowed. She was hyper aware of the noise of metal grinding against asphalt, along with a weird hissing that was coming from the engine. Meanwhile, Lori's arm hurt like a son-of-a-bitch as did her head, which had smacked hard against the window during the initial impact.

Finally, after what seemed an eternity, their SUV came to rest on Ryan's side. Trapped by their seatbelts, Ryan was slumped over the steering wheel. Lori managed to reach a shaking hand over and feel for a pulse. It was there, thank God, though he was out like a light. Sunlight beamed in, blinding her, since her sunglasses had flown off during the rollover. Hazy smoke was curling up from the engine and through the shattered passenger side window. No sirens yet, but they'd surely be on the way soon. A car didn't just roll over and no one noticed. She wondered about the other vehicle. Were the people inside it alive, dead, in the same state?

She winced as she undid her seatbelt, testing the arm trapped beneath her and finding it sore, but able to move without the pain spiking too badly, so not broken then, she didn't think. Good. She needed to get out of here. Needed to get help for Ryan. Needed to let her mom know she was okay. She started to work open her door, only to be stopped by a man in a ski mask with a gun in her face.

Lori just blinked at him a moment, her brain refusing to take it in. Then his hand was on her arm, the sore one, hauling her out of the vehicle and tugging her toward a black van that was waiting nearby. She cried out, trying to reach back for Ryan, trying to get someone to help her at the scene, but there was no one in sight.

"Get in the van," the man holding her said, and through the chaos in her head, she realized she knew that voice. Of course she did. Who else could it be?

"Curtis?" she said, trying to pull away. "What the hell are you doing?"

"Shut up!" He turned back to her, the gun pressed to her abdomen, giving her little choice. "Get in the fucking van or I swear I'll blow your guts out all over this road. Understand?"

His eyes—visible past the mask—were wild, desperate, a far cry from the gaze of the unassuming little nerd she greeted daily on her way up to the office. But then, if she was in the hole to the mob by over a million dollars, she'd be feeling pretty frantic too.

Finally, in the distance, sirens wailed. Help was on the way, at least for Ryan. With an armed Curtis threatening to kill her, she got into the van. He'd tried to off her once already, so she took him seriously now. He zip-tied her hands behind her back, then shoved her roughly inside before slamming the door shut and locking it. Then he ran around and got in behind the wheel and they were off.

It took moment for her eyes to adjust to the darkness. There were no windows back where she was, just shadows. She tried to sit up and realized her crossbody bag was gone, probably left in the car. Good. That way, whoever found Ryan would know she was missing.

As she sat against the side of the van, she realized she still had the other burner phone in her bra. Neal had been right. It might just save her life. If she could figure out a way to use it to get a message to him without Curtis seeing and stopping her.

God, she'd been such an idiot. When he'd asked her to give up her PI work, all she'd pictured was Jordan, trying to steal away her job and her freedom and her reputation. She'd pictured her own mother, broken-hearted in the wake of her divorce, who had had a career-ending affair with her boss back in North Carolina which had been the reason why they'd had to move to Detroit. She'd put all of her old shit and old hang-ups on Neal and their relationship, and all of that had kept her from seeing the reality. Their relationship had problems, yes. But the reason it ended was because she'd chosen to walk away rather than work through them. She hadn't trusted him to support her, to understand her, so she hadn't truly tried to explain. Now, the choice to trust him seemed so obvious that she couldn't believe she'd been holding back all this time. He was her lifeline—literally. To think she'd given him such a hard time about that second phone. Teased him about it. The reassuring weight of the burner phone pressed against her chest like a talisman. All she had to do was figure out how to use it, with her hands secured behind her back.

She couldn't go it alone this time. Didn't want to. She needed Neal.

Lori still stood by her decision not to give in to his ultimatum, but she should have tried harder to find a solution that worked for both of them.

God willing, she'd have a second chance to do that—if she could just get the right message to him in time.

～

Neal was at his dad's house with Lance, still trying to figure out how Curtis had poisoned his father and made it look like a heart attack. They'd found one new candidate for the drug, but it was a long shot, since the substance had to be injected, not swallowed, to be effective. Hard to picture how Curtis would have gotten close enough to their dad to inject him, since Gary Ward had been both paranoid and extremely physically capable. No one got around him.

"Hey," Lance said, scooting back from his desk and snapping his fingers. "What if the stuff in the coffee wasn't poison? What if it was a sedative?"

Neal took that in, frowning as he ran through the case details in his head. "Maybe. The medical examiner's office *did* find non-lethal levels of sleeping pills in Dad's system. I just assumed he'd taken something to help him sleep the night before, like he did sometimes when we were kids."

"Yeah, me too," Lance said, standing to pace the living room. "But what if Curtis put a sedative in Dad's coffee, and that allowed him to get close enough to Dad to inject the real poison?"

The more Neal thought about it, the more it made sense. It might even explain the odd detail of Dad's ring being found on the floor. Curtis could have taken it off, injecting Dad in a spot where the ring would cover the mark, if anyone even bothered to look. But if the dry cleaner had been nervous, as he probably would have been, he might have fumbled the ring, dropping it on the floor. With Lori due to arrive at any moment, he might have decided to leave it rather than crawling under the desk to retrieve it.

Neal instinctively reached for his phone to call Lori and let her know their theory, then stopped. No. They weren't together anymore. She didn't want to hear from him every time an idea popped into his head. He should wait until later, when they were scheduled to meet up at the house, and let her and Ryan know at the same time. That was the mature thing to do. The adult thing. The professional-interactions-only thing.

It just sucked. Big time.

Some of his internal angst must have shown on his face because the next thing Lance said was, "Why exactly did you break up with her again? Because based on your expression right now and hers yesterday, you both are pretty heartbroken about it."

Neal set his phone down on the coffee table and scrubbed a hand over his face. "She's the one who ended it—after I gave her an ultimatum. I had to." He shrugged and sank back into the sofa cushions sullenly. "I couldn't let history repeat itself. Dad always chose the PI agency over us. In the end, it got him killed. I won't make the same mistake again with Lori. If she can't let go of being an investigator, then I just don't see a future for us."

Lance looked at him like he'd grown a second head. "Wait a minute. You think Dad was the way he was because of his work?" He snorted and shook his head. "Shit. I mean, I know you didn't really remember what things were like when Mom was alive, but I guess I thought that you'd figure it out. Obviously I was wrong." He cursed under his breath and plopped down in the armchair across from Neal. "Look, Dad wasn't distant because of the agency. He was like that because of Mom's death."

Now it was Neal's turn to snort. A harsh, derisive sound. "Bullshit. He took up with Ryan's mom barely a year later. That doesn't sound like a broken heart to me. Besides, he even said himself that the work came first. That was always his excuse for missing everything."

Lance gave him a look. "You don't know anything about grief, do you?"

"I know I'd never put my job before my family."

His older brother took a deep breath, then sat back in his chair and stared at the ceiling. "God. I had no idea your view of our childhood was so skewed. I should've talked to you about this before."

"Not your problem," Neal grumbled. He felt pissed and raw and definitely not in the mood to get into all this shit right now. He started to get up. "I need to get to work on—"

"Sit the fuck down," Lance said, his tone brooking no argument. The guy didn't get angry often, but when he did, look out. "We are going to talk about this and we are going to clear the air before you screw up your life even more."

"Hey. I'm not the one divorced and sitting behind a desk at the Pentagon letting the years slip away." Neal regretted the words the moment he said them, but shit. His brother should know not to push him when he was already riled up. Lance's gaze narrowed and a muscle ticked in his cheek near his tight jaw and Neal knew he'd gone too far. "Look, I'm sorry. I—"

Lance sat forward slowly, and Neal wasn't sure if the guy was going to punch him or not. Finally he exhaled slowly and hung his head. No punching, then. "We've both made a mess of things, I guess. But," he looked up at Neal again, "none of that was Dad's fault. He shut down emotionally after Mom's death. It was bad. So bad." His dark brows drew together. "The breast cancer hit her so fast and she was so sick for months before she died. I was only ten then, but even I could see how hard it was on her, on both of them. Dad was never the same after she was gone. He tried for a while, especially after he married Ryan's mom and Ryan was born. He tried to be a good dad, to be there for all of us, but he just couldn't. It was too much. He was too overwhelmed. I think it was just hard for him to be home—to be in all the places where Mom wasn't anymore. The office was better, I guess, because he didn't look up and expect to see her there." Neal opened his mouth to argue, but Lance held up a hand. "And I know he used to say it was because of work, but it wasn't. It was never because of work, Neal. Something in him died along with Mom. His heart was permanently broken. Some wounds stay with you forever. I'd think you of all people would understand that. And I'm not saying he was perfect. He made mistakes. Lots of them. We fought more than once because of them." Lance sighed and sat down again. "Either way, Lori is a different person than Dad. For what it's worth, I don't think she'd ever let grief make her withdraw, and be selfish, and neglect the people she loves like he did."

They sat there in silence for a long while, the only sounds the traffic passing by on the road outside and the tick of the clock on the wall, while Neal tried to wrap his head around what his brother had said. Was Lance right? Had Neal been seeing his childhood through the wrong lens for all these years, blaming the PI firm instead of seeing the true problem?

Another hour went by where both men got back to work, and Neal kept churning the past over and over in his head. Maybe he had judged his father too harshly. If anything happened to Lori, he wasn't sure how he'd deal with it either—and he didn't have two kids at home depending on him for everything. Given his need to protect and take care of people, it was possible Neal would have done the exact same thing his father had. Thrown himself into work, using it as an excuse not to feel all the horrible emotions clawing inside him. He'd already done that a little bit, after all, when he'd been discharged from the SEALs because of his injuries. He'd thrown himself into starting his freelance security. He hadn't really dated or had a social life at all outside of work. A pinch of regret stung his chest. Not for himself, but for just then realizing that maybe he and his dad weren't that different after all.

Neal was just starting to wallow internally over the fact that he was an idiot and that he owed Lori an apology when a text from her came through on his phone. In the quiet living room the buzz sounded louder than normal and he picked the phone up quickly, scowling at his screen.

skipped babysitting to pursue a lead. Meet me at the old bartlemann warehouse in an hour. Come alone.

Uh. That was weird. Lori was crazy about her niece Hope and he was certain she'd never skip a chance to be with the kid, case or no case. Lance's words from just moments before came back to him—Lori wasn't the type to neglect the people she loved. No, this message didn't sound like her at all. Something was off here.

"What's wrong?" Lance asked, glancing back at Neal over his shoulder. "Is it Ryan?"

"No. Not Ryan," Neal said, dialing the number for Lori's mom. She answered on the second ring. "Hey, it's Neal. What time did Lori call you to cancel babysitting this morning?"

"She didn't," Lori's mom said, her tone stressed. "I haven't heard from her at all, which isn't like Lori. What's going on, Neal?"

His gut knotted. He didn't know yet, but he was damned sure going to find out. "Sit tight. I'll let you know as soon as I hear something." He ended the call and met Lance's gaze. "Try to call Ryan."

Lance did, several times. "No answer. Straight to voicemail."

Shit. Shit, shit, shit.

"Something's happened to them," he said, showing Lance the text.

"Either Lori was trying to send you a code or this is a trap," Lance said, handing him back the phone. "What's your plan?"

"To get them back," Neal said, heading for the front door. "Get your service weapon and meet me at the car."

20

―――――

They were about halfway across town to the Bartlemann warehouse when Ryan called Lance's phone. Neal split his concentration between the traffic ahead and his brother in the passenger seat, Lance's phone on speaker so they could both hear.

"Where are you?" Lance said. "What happened?"

"We were in an accident," Ryan said. "I'm just leaving the ER now. I'm fine, but they took Lori."

"Fuck." Neal slammed his hand against the steering wheel. "Did you get a good look at the people who hit you?"

"Nah. We got T-boned out of nowhere—before I even realized what had happened, I was knocked out cold. But I talked to the cops who worked the scene at the ER and they said a witness in one of the houses nearby described a man matching Curtis's description leading Lori away to a black van. They took off and no one knows where they went. No license plate number either."

"Fuck!" Neal said again. It seemed to be all the vocabulary he was capable of at the moment. Anger and regret churned inside him in a caustic sludge. Why had he acted like such an asshole to her? Why had he given her that ultimatum, made her choose between the career she loved and him? If he hadn't been so pig-headed, so stubbornly certain that he was in the right, then he wouldn't have driven her away, and he'd have been there by her side, to keep her safe.

"Hey," Lance said, always the voice of reason. "Beating yourself up and getting lost in your head won't help anyone, Neal. Focus, okay? That text you got said to meet her at the Bartlemann Warehouse. Do you know where that is, Ryan?"

"Yep. Used to sneak in there as a teenager to party. Is that where they took Lori?"

"I think so," Neal said, shaking off his inner turmoil and doing what Lance suggested. Focusing. On the case, on saving Lori. "Listen, can you tell the cops that's where we're going and that there's a possible hostage situation happening there? Lance and I are on our way now. We'll get there first and check it out."

"Will do. Be safe, guys."

"Same, bro. See you soon," Neal said, then ended the call. With traffic snarled ahead, he signaled and turned off onto a side street, thinking back roads might be the faster way to Lori now. All he could think about was Curtis hurting her, and it made him livid. They zoomed through residential neighborhoods and industrial areas, the scenery a blur. Neal disregarded all the posted speed limit signs, intent on rescuing the woman he loved.

Finally, about half an hour later, they pulled up in front of the old, deserted Bartlemann warehouse. Back in the 1940s, it had been used to store metal parts and machinery for the war effort and, later, for the automotive industry. Now, it was just a vast, hollow shell of its former glory, all broken windows and creaking doors. The metal walls of the building had rusted through in spots and grass grew up through jagged cracks in the concrete floor.

"Shit. That's enormous," Lance said, getting out of the car to stare at the huge, hulking monstrosity in front of them. He wasn't wrong. Neal remembered reading that the old warehouse was at least three football fields long and two stories high. There'd been talk by the city of Detroit at one time about turning it into some kind of multi-use public space with shops and offices and stuff, but actual plans had never materialized. Lance shook his head. "There's no way we can search that place with just the two of us."

Dammit. His brother was right. Neal walked over and peered down one side of the long building, then the other, hoping maybe to catch sight of the black van that had been used to abduct Lori from the accident scene, but no such luck.

"We should wait for the police," Lance said when Neal returned to his side. "That way, we'll have enough manpower to search the whole place at once and can cut off Curtis's escape routes."

It sounded reasonable enough, but Neal couldn't do it. "No. I don't want to not show up when Curtis told me to. I have no idea what he'd do to Lori if he thought I wasn't cooperating. I won't take that chance." He checked his watch. It had taken longer to get here than he'd anticipated, going the back way, and now there was less than five minutes left until the deadline. "I can't wait."

He'd just pulled out his service weapon from the holster at his waist to click off the safety, when his phone buzzed in his pocket again. Heart in his throat, he pulled it out with his free hand, and his pulse tripped at what he saw.

It was another text from Lori, sharing the same location. This text was different than the first, listing more precisely where they were in the warehouse and what weapons Curtis had on him. It also told Neal what traps Curtis had set up inside the warehouse for them along the way.

The biggest difference was where it had been sent from. The first text had come from the replacement phone he'd gotten for Lori after the fire in the office, the one she kept in her purse. This second one, though, had come from the second burner phone number. The one she'd fought him on, but that he'd insisted she carry with her at all times for emergencies. The knowledge that he'd done something right and that his planning had given her something she was using now to contact him made an odd mix of urgency and joy swell inside him. It was short-lived, however—the joy part anyway—when he got a second text from Lori at the same number, saying that Curtis had left her alone for a moment, but she had no idea how long he'd be gone.

Jesus.

His SEAL instincts were going haywire. Part of him wanted to run right in there and swoop down on Curtis King Kong style, beat him to a pulp for what he'd done, and carry Lori away in his arms. But the rest of him knew that no matter how real it sounded, this could still be a trap. He had to make certain first before charging into danger.

He typed in a fast response, his thumbs flying over the phone screen.

Tell me something only Lori would know.

A pause. Those three little dots flashing for what felt like a small eternity, letting him know the other person was typing their message. Then a response, one that made his pulse trip all over again, for the best of reasons.

I don't accept our break-up. rescue me so I can tell you why you're wrong.

"What's going on?" Lance asked as Neal laughed. "What is it?"

"I'm going in," Neal said, chambering a round and heading for the rusted doors at the front of the warehouse. "Stay here and wait for Ryan and the cops."

"Neal," Lance started, then shook his head. "Fine. Just be careful."

"Always," Neal called back, then squeezed through a crack in the doors that refused to budge. Inside, it took a second for his eyes to adjust. The air smelled stale and dusty and narrow shafts of hazy sunlight streaked the walls in spots. There was the occasional squeak or groan of metal on metal, but nothing that sounded human. Old machinery squatted around the perimeter of the warehouse floor, forgotten and unused, and the occasional safety sign hung crooked on the walls. Large steel girders supported the ceiling, and dust motes floated in the beams of light streaming in from the outside. Weapon drawn and raised, he began making his way slowly down the length of the warehouse toward a rickety, rust-splotched staircase to the second floor at the opposite end of the place, careful to avoid the spots where Lori had said Curtis set up traps for them.

Quiet and stealthy, he made his way to the staircase, then up, keeping his back to the wall and his gun aimed upward toward the second floor. Lori had said that Curtis had left her alone, which meant he could be anywhere up here, but when Neal reached the top of the stairs, it was just more empty space. He'd just started down the hall toward the room where Lori was being held, according to her text, when a sound behind him made him swivel around fast, finger poised over the trigger of his weapon.

Lance stood there, hands raised, his service weapon in one of them. "It's me. Sorry. But there was no way in hell I was letting you face this alone, brother."

Chest tight, Neal managed to take a much-needed deep breath before lowering his weapon. "I could've shot your ass."

His brother grinned and moved to his side. "Yeah, but you didn't. Now, come on. Let's get Lori."

Together, they made their way down the rest of the hallway to the corner room. Once they'd flanked the door on each side, Neal raised a finger to his lips for silence, then on the count of three, kicked in the old metal door to find Lori huddled in the corner. He rushed over and knelt down beside her, blood pounding behind his temples.

"Shit, darlin'. I was so worried about you," he whispered, cupping her cheeks. "Are you okay?"

She nodded, then winced. "I'm mostly fine. Just a little sore from the accident and those stupid zip ties he used on my wrists on the way over here." Lori held his wrists. "You need to hurry. I don't know when he's coming back."

Neal let her go and focused on undoing the thick, heavy rope around her ankle, which was tethered to a steel bolt in the floor. The easiest way to get her out of it would be to cut it, but all he had with him was his Swiss army knife which wasn't that big. Still, one of the lessons he'd learned as a SEAL was making do with what you had, so he pulled out the smaller blade and began sawing through the rope, careful to avoid Lori's delicate skin, while Lance stood guard out in the hall.

He'd gotten about halfway through the thick hemp when the distant wail of sirens grew closer. Good. Help was on the way. Lance moved farther out into the hall, pulling out his phone, probably to text Ryan. Neal focused on the rope again. "Almost there, darlin'. Almost free."

"Oh my God," Lori said, jerking under his hands. "Look out!"

Neal looked up just in time to see the shadow of a weapon slide across Lance's back. He acted on pure instinct, dropping the knife in his hand and grabbing his sidearm arm in one smooth move. The shot was fired as Curtis stepped into view in the doorway, a perfect shot to the leg, felling the guy without taking him completely out. Neal wanted to question the motherfucker before he rotted away in prison, find out why Curtis had killed his dad, why he'd gone after the woman Neal loved more than anything in the world. Death wasn't good enough for the likes of Curtis Hill. Not yet, anyway.

"Shit." Lance turned fast, tucking away his phone, then kneeling beside a writhing Curtis on the floor. "Thanks for covering me," he said to Neal, and quickly examined Curtis's wound. Then he looked at Neal again, his expression grim.

"What?" Neal asked. "I took out his leg."

"You nicked his femoral artery," Lance said, pulling off his T-shirt to apply pressure to the wound. "He'll bleed out before the cops arrive."

"Fuck." It had been a split-second move. Shoot first, ask questions later, but shit. He'd tried to aim for a non-lethal location but had missed the mark. While Lance provided emergency first aid, Neal pulled out his phone and called Ryan, filling him in on what happened and getting an ETA on the ambulance, wincing at the answer his brother gave him. According to Ryan, the ambulance was still twenty minutes out, due to traffic. So yeah. Curtis was a goner. Neal had seen enough of those types of wounds in battle to know they didn't have much time at all. Maybe fifteen minutes tops, if the guy was lucky. And considering he'd been shot, Curtis didn't seem lucky today.

Neal finished cutting Lori free, then walked over to where Lance was still putting pressure on Curtis's leg. Not that it was doing much good, as blood continued to pour out from the gunshot wound, pooling beneath Curtis's body. Neal knelt down carefully beside the dying man and stared down into his face. "You're not going to make it, Curtis. I'd say you have maybe ten minutes left to live, five of which you'll be conscious for. Do you really want to take all that guilt to your grave? There's a special place in hell, Curtis, for people who kill other people. Did you know that?"

Curtis was shaking and pale from the blood loss already. His pulse was probably racing too at this point, Neal knew from his training, as his vascular system constricted to try and compensate for the lower blood volume, but it was too late. Outside the sirens grew closer, but not close enough for Curtis.

It almost made Neal feel sorry for the guy. Almost.

"Tell me why you murdered my father, Curtis," he said, keeping his voice deliberately low and flat. "We already know you gave him a sedative in his coffee, so you could get close enough to inject him with poison. What we don't know is why. Why did you kill Gary Ward, Curtis?" He turned the imaginary screws tighter, trying to force the man to tell him the truth, to guilt it out of him, if possible. "He was your friend. A business associate. He trusted you, Curtis. You saw each other every day in the lobby. Said hello. Maybe shared building gossip or a doughnut now and then. Why would you kill him?"

"I—" Curtis coughed, the sound wet and phlegmy.

Lori moved in beside Neal. "Curtis, did someone force you to do this? To make you pay off a debt? We know about your gambling problem. And I also know that this wasn't like you. If someone forced you into this, then telling us now might be your last chance to make them pay for what they've done. They can't hurt you anymore—you don't have any reason to be afraid. So now's the time to do the right thing. Please, Curtis. Tell us the truth about what happened to Gary."

A moment's hesitation, then Curtis spilled the whole thing, talking fast to beat the clock, his tone rushed and reedy, like a balloon draining of air. "They blackmailed and threatened me into killing Gary. I didn't want to do it, but they said they'd kill me. Kill everyone I loved."

"Who, Curtis?" Lori asked, placing her hand on his cold, gray one. "Who did this to you?"

"T-the m-mob," he whispered. "But I screwed it up. I didn't know what I was doing. I forgot to take the coffee cup with me when I left. A-and when I took off Gary's ring so I could inject him where no one would see it, I couldn't get the damned ring back on." He gasped for breath, his gaze going wild, darting between Neal and Lori and Lance before landing and staying on Lori. "I saw you coming, through the window, and I knew I had to get out of there. So I dropped the ring and ran." He winced, his body contracting on itself in pain. "Didn't r-remember until later that the cup and ring had my fingerprints on them. So s-stupid. S-so fu-fucking s-stupid."

Lori and Neal exchanged a look.

"I t-tried to get you to d-drop the case," Curtis said, shudders racking his body harder now as his shock deepened. "B-but you w-wouldn't let it go. Then I t-thought the o-only w-way out was to k-kill you and N-neal."

Neal exhaled slowly, blinking down at the dying man. "Did you tell the mob? About how you screwed up? Do they know that Lori and I are on the case?"

Curtis shook his head. "N-no. I w-was t-too s-scared."

Lance looked over at Neal. "We can use this. If they don't know about his mistakes, then we have the upper hand. We can go after the person who ordered the hit on Dad and they won't see us coming."

Neal nodded. It sounded good on paper, but there were still a lot of things left to work out. But for now, he'd take what he could get. For starters, that meant the comfort of knowing that no one else was targeting Lori. Once Curtis was gone, she'd finally be safe. This wasn't how he'd wanted the situation to play out, but there was still some relief to be found in it.

The sirens reached the warehouse and within minutes, the second floor was swarming with cops and EMTs. Ryan was there too, looking a bit beat up from his accident, but not seriously impaired. Curtis was unconscious now and Neal doubted the guy would ever wake up again. They each gave their statements to the police, about how Curtis had caused the accident earlier, then kidnapped Lori from the scene, how Neal had shot Curtis in self-defense and how Curtis had confessed to murdering their father.

The only part they left out was why.

21

———

"Well, maybe that accident finally knocked some sense into you," Lance said from the backseat of Neal's car, where he was seated next to Ryan.

"Ha. Ha. So my concussion is funny to you?" Ryan gave his oldest brother a look.

"No." Lance took a deep breath. "I'm glad you're okay."

"Even if you did sleep through Lori getting abducted," Neal chimed in from behind the wheel.

Lori knew they were just kidding around, but she didn't like them ganging up on Ryan. She reached over and punched Neal lightly on the arm, wincing slightly as her sore shoulder pulled. They'd just left the hospital where all of them had been checked out, Ryan for the second time. Her shoulder was bruised and slightly strained, but nothing torn or broken, thank goodness. And Ryan's concussion was minor too, though the staff did go over protocol with Lance to keep an eye on him that night and bring him back in if there were any problems. "Leave him alone."

Neal glanced at her and then back at the road, chuckling. "I guess things could've been worse."

That was the understatement of the century.

They'd all come away from the day's events with only minor injuries at most. That was very lucky indeed in Lori's book. Especially considering that Curtis Hill was dead.

"So, what's up next?" Ryan asked after a beat or two.

"What do you mean?" Neal asked. "It's over."

"No." Lance scowled. "It's not over."

They stopped at a red light and all eyes focused on the eldest Ward brother.

"I'll be handling the next stage of this investigation," Lance continued, his voice deathly serious.

"Why?" Ryan asked at the same time Lori and Neal did.

"Because Curtis never mentioned tailing Neal and Lori at the mall."

Lori considered that a moment. "Maybe not, but he was pretty out of it back there. He'd lost a lot of blood and he knew he only had a few minutes to talk, so I'm sure some details were left out."

"But you'd have recognized him if it was Curtis tailing you that day, right?"

Shit. Lori hadn't thought of that. She sat back, the bubble of satisfaction at having solved a case bursting inside her, only to be replaced by a niggle of unease. The mob had been involved, which meant this case went far deeper than just finding Gary's killer. They still needed to find the person who had ordered his death. They needed to solve the mystery Gary had died chasing. She felt she owed that much to Gary. From the look on Lance's face, he was feeling much the same way.

She sighed. "It was crowded that day, so it was hard to see everyone there, but yeah. If he'd been there, I would've recognized him."

"So what are you saying, then?" Neal frowned, turning back forward as the light turned green. He accelerated through the intersection, heading back toward Gary's house to drop off Lance and Ryan. "You think the mob sent someone else after us?"

"Not sure." Lance shook his head and stared out the window beside him. "All I know is that you two weren't tailed until after you talked to my ex-wife, Ruth. And I'd bet good money that means she really was the client behind the case that got Dad killed. Those mysterious heart attack deaths Dad mentioned in the voicemail to Neal? Those must have been Ruth's clients—the ones she had Dad look into."

"Holy shit," Ryan said.

"Exactly." Lance exhaled slowly. "I want to know why the hell she wasn't open with you two when you went to talk to her about the case. Especially if she's in danger. And I want to know if she's aware that the mafia is watching her closely enough to know when she takes an unexpected meeting with her ex-brother-in-law."

Neal nodded, then glanced in the rear-view mirror to meet his older brother's eyes. "That's a good reason for you to take things from here."

"It is," Ryan conceded. "I guess since you were married to Ruth once upon a time, that gives you dibs."

"Okay, first of all," Lori said, unable to stand the caveman logic any longer, "the level of testosterone in this car is making you all say stupid crap. Ruth is an attorney and one of the smartest people I know. If she didn't tell us something, I'm sure there's a good reason for it." She shifted slightly to look around the seat at Lance. "And second, I'm the one with the PI license here. So you can take point on the investigation if you want, I'll give you that. But you still need to report in to me every step of the way to keep this all above-board and legal. Got it?"

For a moment, Lance looked like he wanted to argue, but finally he gave her a curt nod. As did the other Ward brothers. In her line of work, she was used to dealing with difficult men. In fact, Gary always said it was one of her fortes.

They reached Gary's house and Lance and Ryan got out. Neal put the car in park and unfastened his seatbelt, looking over at Lori. "Be right back. I just need to talk to them real quick about something."

He leaned over and kissed her fast, then was out of the vehicle before she could respond. She just blinked at him through the window as he and his brothers stood on the sidewalk in front the house. Her lips tingled and her heart ached. They still had a lot to talk about, but she missed him. She wanted him back in her life, however she could get him. Hopefully, they could work this all out.

Then Neal was back in the car, kissing her again before fastening his seatbelt and taking off for her house. He was smiling broadly, like the cat with a canary, and she just hoped that whatever it was that was making him grin like that would be good for both of them.

When they got back to her house, she and Neal went their separate ways to shower and change, meeting up again in the kitchen about an hour later. She was dying of anticipation, wanting to know what was happening with their relationship, but at the same time dreading what the answer might be.

It was entirely possible he felt exactly the same way he did before—that they could only be together if she would agree to give up her job for him. If he stuck with that ultimatum, she'd do everything in her power to change his mind…except for giving up her job. But she hated to shatter the calm, comfortable mood that had descended over them as they prepared dinner together. Or, rather, Neal prepared dinner and Lori set the table and chopped some veggies for a salad.

In the end, though, Neal was the one who brought it up while he stirred a pot of yummy-smelling pasta sauce on the stove. "What exactly did you mean by 'I'm not accepting our break-up'?"

The casualness of his tone caught her off-guard, and she set her sharp knife aside with trembling fingers before she lost a digit. Fine. Okay. It was now or never. Best to get it all out there now so they could talk about it instead of letting it fester. She took a deep breath for courage, then said, "I'm not going to change careers because you say so, Neal. I'm firm on that. Non-negotiable. But," she wiped her hands on a dish towel, then rested a hip on the edge of the counter as she turned to face him. "I am willing to listen to your concerns and figure out a plan so that you feel secure and happy in our relationship. I'm not choosing the job over you—I'm choosing to have both." Lori tossed the towel aside. "Hell, we can even do therapy if you want. Whatever it takes. Because I'm not giving up PI work. I love it too much and I've worked too hard to get here."

He didn't respond. Just kept stirring that pot, and damn, she couldn't resist touching him any longer. She walked up behind him and wrapped her arms around his waist, squeezing tight and burying her face in his back, inhaling his good Neal smell.

"I won't walk away from you either, though," she said, her voice muffled by his T-shirt.

Neal inhaled deeply, then set his spoon aside and turned to face her. His expression was unreadable, but she took some comfort in the way he didn't try to step out of her embrace. Instead, he folded his hands behind her lower back, looking down at her. "Thanks for that. I appreciate your honesty. But you should know that Lance told me it wasn't the agency that was the problem with my dad after all. Burying himself in work was how he handled his grief after losing my mom.

The job wasn't really the problem—it was just his excuse. And you're a different person than he was, Lori. You'd never push away your loved ones like that."

"True," she said, pulse pounding and chest constricted. If he was going to leave her once and for all, she wished he'd get on with it, because the suspense was killing her. "But?"

She sensed there was a "but". Seemed there was always a "but" where she was concerned. Her hopes faltered.

He sighed. "But I also think part of the problem is that running the agency alone is way too much for one person."

Also true, though she didn't say that out loud.

"Which is why I have a different idea now for your job, somewhere between you taking the non-PI position at my friend's company that I found for you and you buying out my dad's agency."

"Okay," Lori said, having no idea where this was headed now.

"I want you to run Ward Investigations with me. Equal partners. Fifty-fifty."

She'd heard the expression "knock someone over with a feather" before, but that was the first time it had ever applied to her. Knees wobbly, she let Neal go and sank into a chair at the kitchen table, her mind whirling.

He must have taken her actions as a no because next thing Lori knew, Neal was crouching beside her, taking her hands in his, his gaze earnest. "Please, Lori. At least consider it. I just talked to my brothers about it when I dropped them off, and they agreed. But if you don't want to run the agency together, then I'll convince them to turn it over to you while I try to transfer my business here to Detroit. And we can look into finding another partner for you—someone you think is the right fit. I just know that I love working with you and I don't want to go anywhere. If you say yes, then we'll get the agency back up and running again full tilt. That way Lance and Ryan can go after the mob who killed Dad full time."

Lori blinked at him, stunned speechless for the first time in forever. It was like he'd read her heart and was offering her everything she'd ever wanted. But was it too good to be true? She'd felt the same way about Jordan once upon a time, and look where that had gotten her. But Neal was no Jordan. He was so much better. He was the best person she'd ever known, actually. And she loved him with all her heart and soul. She'd be a fool to turn him down.

Before she could say that to him, though, he plowed on ahead, his obvious nervousness adorable.

"And I know you said you'd never date anyone you worked with because of that asshole who betrayed you, but this time would be different, Lori. I swear. We'd each have equal power and ownership of the company. No hidden agendas. No secrets." Neal swallowed hard and met her gaze. "So, what do you say? Do you trust me enough to go into business with me?"

Lori nodded, blinking back tears. "Yes. Of course I trust you, Neal. But there's something else I need to know first." She cupped his cheeks, savoring his warmth and the scrape of his stubble on her skin. "Do you love *working* with me, or do you love *me*?"

A beat passed, then two, as he stared at her. Then he smiled, the same wide grin he'd had earlier in the car. The same one that made her pulse trip and her insides buzz with joy. "Both."

"Good." She was grinning now too. And crying. "Because I love both too—for you."

Then they were kissing, her kneeling on the floor with him, and today went from being an ending to a new beginning. One filled with love

and hope and family and all the things that were truly important in
life.

EPILOGUE

One week later…

"This space will go fast, folks," the real estate agent said, showing them around a potential spot for their new Ward Investigation offices. "Restored historic building, great midtown location, first floor walk-out, close to public transit. I've given several tours already and have a couple clients considering making an offer on this one. If you're interested, I'd suggest moving fast."

"Uh," Neal said, holding Lori's hand. "Could we, um, have a minute? Look around by ourselves?"

"Sure thing," the agent said, pulling her buzzing cell phone from her pocket. "I'll be outside if you need me."

"Great." Neal waited until the door closed behind the agent, then walked with Lori through the open concept office area. It was certainly bright and airy, with white walls, exposed brick, and lovely herringbone hardwood floors. There was plenty of foot traffic, too, from the busy sidewalk outside and also from the apartment dwellers living in the floors above them. Of all the places they'd toured so far, this one seemed pretty perfect to Neal. "What do you think?"

"I like it," Lori said, the wonder on her face as she looked around confirming the fact.

Honestly, when she had that look on her face, the place could have been covered in soot and smelled like a sewer for all Neal cared. He only had eyes for her. Later that night they were going on their first real romantic, no-one-is-trying-to-kill-us date and he had a very special gift he wanted to give her then. He'd been carrying it around in his pocket for days, the small weight of the tiny velvet box making him giddy in all the silliest of ways. He was a fucking SEAL, for Christ's sake. He didn't get giddy.

Except when Lori was around.

She let go of his hand and wandered over to a staircase that led down to a basement storage area, Neal guessed. Lori disappeared down-stairs, then called up to him a moment later. "Neal, come here. You need to see this!"

Her excitement was palpable and contagious. He went down the stairs and stopped at the bottom. He'd been right. It was storage, partially anyway. But there was also an awesome break area, complete with a kitchenette and seating for up to eight people at a time, plus another set of private bathrooms for the staff, and a small space for a sofa and maybe a TV, if they wanted. It was perfect.

She was perfect.

Aw, screw it. He was giving her the gift now. After all, one of the things he was working on with Lori was being more spontaneous, instead of always working with a plan A, B, and C like he had in the past. *Carpe diem* and all that shit.

He walked over to where she was still ohh-ing and ahh-ing over the stainless-steel appliances in the kitchenette and wrapped his arms around her from behind, pulling her back into his chest. "Close your eyes and hold out your hands," he whispered near her ear, loving the way she shivered against him. When she complied, he took the small, square velvet box out of his jacket pocket and placed it in her palms. "Okay. You can open them."

Lori gasped, turned toward him, then gasped again. "What did you do?"

"Open it," he said again.

His heart thudded, hoping she'd like what he picked. He was hardly a jewelry expert, but the man at the store had asked him some questions about Lori and their relationship, then helped him pick out something he thought would be appropriate. Now, though, Neal was nervous. He wanted her to like it.

Please, let her like it.

She creaked the lid of the box open and smiled, and damn if it wasn't like the sun coming out on a cloudy day. Neal's whole universe brightened at the delight on her face. "Oh my gosh. Neal, this is gorgeous." She held up the necklace, the antique diamond and sapphire pendant sparkling beneath the overhead lights. "Where did you find this?"

He shrugged, feeling warm in all the best ways. "Martin Antique Jewelers, over on North Calvert. I wanted to get you something unique and one of a kind because that's what you are to me. A special treasure."

"Oh, sweetie." She walked over and kissed him, slow and sweet, then leaned back to look at the necklace again, this time more closely. "Martin Jewelers, you said? Huh. You know, about a year ago there was a big jewelry store heist here in town. All over the news. Most of the stuff was never recovered. Lots of it was very old and very valuable. I wonder…"

Lori squinted and frowned at the necklace and Neal's heart dropped.

"No," he said.

"What?" She smiled again, this time more slyly. "I'm not saying this was part of that heist, but I'm not saying it wasn't, either. Think about it," she said, off and running, her PI brain not shutting off for a second. "If this was part of that crime and now we know which jewelry shop it ended up in, we could work backward to find out who did it!"

Neal shook his head and threw up his hands, exasperated. "I give up. And I am never buying you anything but brand-new jewelry again, woman!"

"Aw, come on." She giggled. "Where's the fun in that?"

He sighed and pulled her into his arms again, laughing. "Can't we just enjoy the moment, eh? Before we start working on our next case?"

"So, you're saying we can investigate it, yes?"

"Fine. Yes!" He kissed her, then kissed her again before resting his forehead against hers. "First, though, what are we doing about this place? Should we get it?"

"I think we should," she said, smiling. "It's everything I wanted."

"For now?" he asked, pulling her closer. "Or forever?"

"Definitely forever," Lori said, rising up on tiptoe to press her lips to his, and Neal got the feeling they were talking about way more than office space. At least he was. With Lori, he never felt like a second choice. He loved her more than anything on earth and it was both humbling and joyful to know that she'd chosen him first, same as he'd done with her. Same as he would continue to do as long as she wanted him.

He kissed her again, deeper and hotter, then pulled back, breathless and ready, so ready, for whatever their future held. "Definitely forever indeed."

END OF SEAL'S PRETEND GIRLFRIEND
WARD INVESTIGATION BOOK ONE

SEAL's Pretend Girlfriend, March 24, 2022

SEAL's Pregnant Ex-Wife, March 31, 2022

SEAL's Fake Relationship, April 7, 2022

PS: Do you like sexy military men? Then keep reading for exclusive extracts from ***SEAL's Pregnant Ex-Wife, His Stubborn Lover*** and ***SEAL's Homecoming.***

THANK YOU!

Thank you so much for purchasing my book. It's hard for me to put into words how much I appreciate my readers. If you enjoyed this book, please remember to leave a review. Reviews are crucial for an author's success and I would greatly appreciate it if you took the time to review the book. I love hearing from you!

You can connect with me on:

goodreads.com/leslienorth

bookbub.com/authors/leslie-north

facebook.com/leslienorthbooks

x.com/leslienorthbook

THANK YOU

ABOUT LESLIE

Leslie North is the USA Today Bestselling pen name for a critically-acclaimed author of women's contemporary romance and fiction. The anonymity gives her the perfect opportunity to paint with her full artistic palette, especially in the romance and erotic fantasy genres.

Find your next Leslie North book visit LeslieNorthBooks.com or choose:

BY TROPE

BY HERO

PS: Want sneak peeks, giveaways, ARC offers, fun extras and plenty of pictures of bad boys? Join my Facebook group, Leslie's Lovelies!

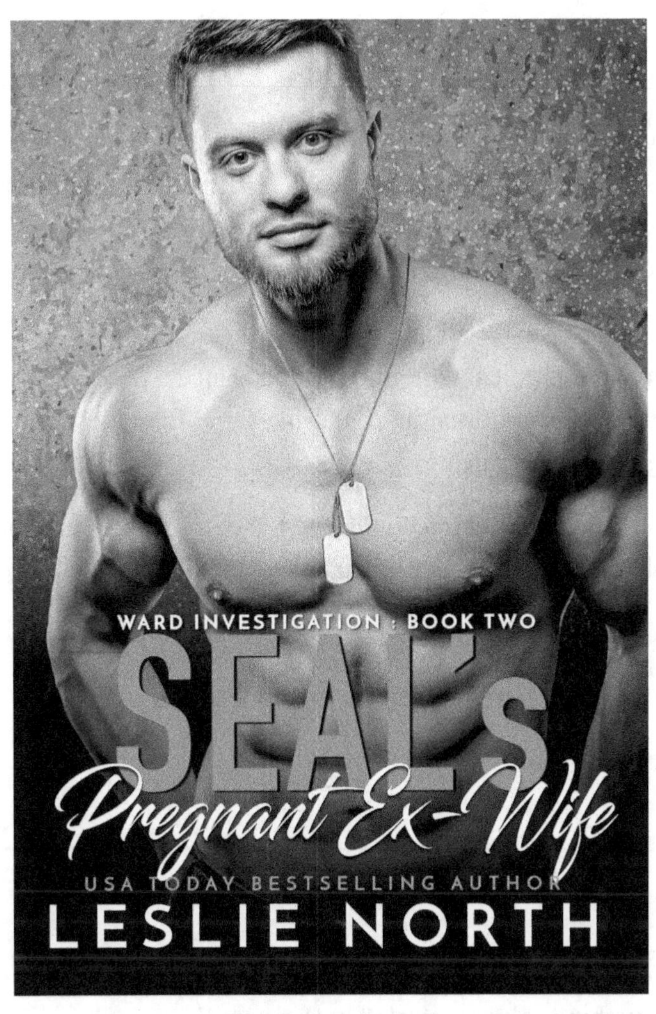

BLURB

This Navy SEAL knows danger… but it's nothing compared to fighting to regain true love.

Navy SEAL Lance Ward never thought he'd be in the position of seducing his ex-wife and protecting their unborn child—all while trying to solve his father's murder. Yet, here he is, thanks to Ruth, the only woman who knows how to get under his skin—and under his clothes—in record time. The only problem is, Ruth has zero interest in getting back together. But he's not so keen on letting her go a second time.

Ruth gave up on a happily ever after a long time ago. She's not the same naïve young woman she was when she married Lance all those years ago. These days, she's a successful, hard-hitting lawyer… with a soft spot for a certain SEAL who can make her blood sing—and for their unborn child.

But Ruth's in a predicament. She'd hired Lance's father to investigate suspicious deaths and then he'd met the same fate. Now it looks like the bad guys are after her.

As danger nears and her feelings for Lance burn brighter than ever, Ruth realizes it's not just her life at risk… but her heart.

**Grab your copy of *SEAL's Pregnant Ex-Wife*
www.LeslieNorthBooks.com**

~

EXCERPT

Chapter One

Funny how things always circled back around.

Lance Ward got out of his car and stood on the sidewalk in front of a bland-looking office building in downtown Detroit, and took a deep breath. The air smelled crisp and clear with a hint of water from the nearby river. Sun was shining today, though the shadows from the buildings blocked out most of it here. Two months ago, he'd wondered if he'd ever come home again.

Now he was back, with a mission. A personal mission he needed to handle in the next three weeks.

He looked both ways, then jogged across the busy street to the entrance. The place was a little worn and dated, but still functional—and it seemed to be fully occupied. The lobby was full of suits rushing this way and that.

God, he hated these kinds of spaces.

Give him open air and blue skies any day over stuffy boring offices.

It was one of the things he missed most about being boots on the ground with his SEAL team.

Which made the fact he was now stuck working in one of those stuffy boring offices himself these days that much more ironic. And awful. The fact that the office building happened to be the Pentagon didn't make it any more appealing. But he had three more weeks of personal leave away from it, during which he had a job to do, a mystery to solve. It involved his late father, his family, and the woman he was here to see today—his ex-wife, Ruth Becker.

After his father, Gary, had died unexpectedly, Lance and his brothers had struggled to come to terms with the loss—right up until Gary's assistant-turned-partner at his PI business had come forward with her theory: that Gary was murdered. Eventually, they had caught the killer…but then learned that Gary's murder was tied to a larger organization. One that might have set its sights on Ruth, who had hired Gary for the investigation that eventually led to his death. And that was why Lance was here now: because he feared she might be in ongoing danger.

An elevator dinged and he hurried over to get onboard with the others. He pressed the button for the fifth floor and then stood in the corner, a good head taller than anyone else in the car with him. Everyone stared straight forward as they jolted upward.

Soon, he exited the elevator again onto beige carpets that led to a door reading *Becker Law LLC*.

Passing through the door, he found himself faced with a reception desk. He approached, putting on his best charming smile. "Hello, I'd like to see Ruth Becker, please."

The woman behind the desk glanced up from her computer and did a double-take. Lance didn't think much about how he looked, but women seemed to like it and it came in handy at times like this. He'd inherited his height from his dad, as had his two brothers, and they all shared his dark brown curly hair, too. Then the navy had had twenty years to tone and shape him into someone capable of completing any task—even charming his way into a meeting with his ex. He batted his green eyes at the woman openly ogling him now, not above a little flirting if it got him what he needed.

"Is she available?" he asked when the woman didn't respond, leaning an elbow on the desk and widening his smile a bit more, lowering his voice to sound a bit naughtier.

The woman frowned and clicked more keys on her computer. "Name, please?"

"Lance Ward." He straightened a bit. "I don't have an appointment."

"Oh. Um." Pink flushed the woman's cheeks and her frown deepened. "Then I'm sorry, but I'm afraid Ms. Becker is—"

"We're old friends," he said, which was true, if misleading. She'd been his best friend when he'd married her at age eighteen. The friendship had mostly fizzled out after she asked for a divorce when they were twenty-two—he'd been too busy feeling shocked and hurt and discarded to feel all that friendly—but even in the aftermath, their relationship had never been bitter or harsh. They'd just…continued their lives in separate directions, right up until his father's funeral, when he saw her for the first time in years. He gave the woman a look, one that crinkled the corners of his eyes, then winked. "She'll see me."

"One moment, please." The woman swiveled her chair away and picked up the phone receiver to call Ruth. Her tone was too quiet for him to hear much of what was said, but pretty soon the woman hung up and gave Lance a curt nod. "Please have a seat. She'll be with you shortly."

"Thanks." He'd barely made it two steps before a familiar voice echoed from behind him.

"What are you doing here?" Ruth said.

He turned to find her standing outside a doorway down the hall to his right, looking as lovely as ever. He walked over to her, ignoring the receptionist's curious stare following him, and stopped outside her office door where Ruth stood with her arms crossed over the top of her gray blazer. "Uh, hi. Sorry to stop by like this, but we need to talk."

Her dark eyes looked wary. She waited until he got closer to her to whisper, "Is this about our hook-up?"

Damn. Lance had been doing his best to forget that for the past couple of weeks.

God. What the fuck had he been thinking? Well, he hadn't. That was the problem. It had been the day after his dad's funeral. Lance had been wrecked, physically and emotionally. He and his dad had had their share of issues. No lie. But they'd slowly been reconnecting these past few years, talking once a week on the phone about sports and work and other assorted stuff that didn't mean anything really, and everything too, all at the same time. So when he'd gotten the call that Gary was dead, completely out of the blue, it had hit Lance hard. Harder than he'd ever expected.

Then, seeing Ruth again at the funeral, had been… wow. She'd seemed like a ray of light in an otherwise gray, dreary world, and he'd been drawn to her once more like a moth to the proverbial flame.

When she'd invited him for a drink the day after the funeral, he'd been compelled to accept. And later, when they'd gone back to her place, falling into bed with her and losing himself in her body felt like a balm to his wounded soul. The way she'd felt under him, around him. The way she smelled, tasted, sounded. So familiar, yet so very new and exciting too after the time apart. It had been like coming home and discovering it all over again.

Focus, dude. Focus.

Lance shook off the memories of their night together and cleared his throat. "It's not about that."

"Too bad," she said with a ghost of a smile. "I had a good time. But you're right. Best to forget about it. But if not that, why are you here? Come to think of it, why are you still in Detroit at all? I thought you went back to DC already."

"I did. My boss needed me to come back for two weeks to handle some things that couldn't wait, in exchange for more time off now. I'm back because there's more going on connected to my father's death—and I won't be leaving until I get to the bottom of it. That's why I'm here. To talk about your meeting with Neal and Lori a few weeks ago."

The color drained from Ruth's pretty face and she blinked up at him a second, then stepped back to wave him inside her office. He didn't miss the way her gaze darted in both directions before she followed him inside and shut the door. Yep. Something was definitely up here. Ruth had a secret, and he was going to find out what.

"I don't know what you want me to say, Lance," she said, not looking at him now as she took a seat back behind her desk. "It was a short meeting, Neal and Lori following up on why I decided to drop my investigation. Why would we need to talk about that?"

"Because I want to know why you lied to my brother and Lori," Lance said gently. Neal had told him that Ruth had seemed spooked during their interview, which had happened just a few days after the funeral. She looked shaken now, too. She'd told Neal at the time that she hadn't gotten any threats connected to the case she'd given Gary…but Neal hadn't believed her, and Lance didn't, either. She was in danger, and she knew it. So why was she lying about it? Didn't she know he'd do anything to help her, protect her?

"I didn't lie. I told them exactly what I'm going to repeat to you now. I hired Gary to double check some facts for me because I suspected my clients were being dishonest with me. I do that a lot. It's routine in my field."

He sighed and stretched out his long legs, making himself comfortable, not intending to budge any time soon as he dropped another bombshell. "Ruth, I'm sure you've seen the papers—you know my dad was murdered and that my brothers and I caught the killer. But what the police kept out of the papers was that the killer was just the trigger man. My dad was poisoned on orders from someone in the mob—poisoned in such a way as to make it look like a heart attack. And we believe it happened while he was investigating the deaths of other people who might also have been poisoned in the same way." She froze and he knew he'd hit a bullseye. He leaned in, holding eye contact with her for this next part, the part he really wanted her to pay attention to. "When Neal and Lori left your office after talking to you, they were tailed. It was *not* by Gary's killer. We have reason to believe it was someone connected to the mob. That was the one and only time they were followed by someone other than the killer, which makes it seem pretty obvious to us that the mob wasn't keeping an eye on them—it was keeping an eye on *you.* And it might still be."

He paused for a minute, letting her absorb all of that. Then he spoke again. "I suspect there's a lot more to this story than what you're telling me. And I think you need to tell me exactly what happened that led to you hiring my dad, and what made you call Lori off and cancel the investigation after he was killed. This isn't going away, Ruth. And if you ignore that—if you refuse to tell me what happened, refuse to let me help—it might just get you killed."

"Lance, I'm—"

"I don't want to see anything happen to you. That's why I'm here. Jesus, Ruth." Lance stood, needing to burn off some of the energy pinballing inside him. "You were always so strong. Strong and brave and determined to do the right thing. Those were some of the things I lov—" He stopped himself before he said the words. It had been too long and there'd been too much water under the bridge to go back there again. Not now. Maybe not ever. He raked a hand through his hair and stared at the books on her shelves until his pulse slowed. Dammit. He needed to get this right. For his dad. For his family. For himself. And for her.

Grab your copy of *SEAL's Pregnant Ex-Wife*
www.LeslieNorthBooks.com

His Stubborn Lover

Blurb

Never mix business with pleasure…

Keira Mantz just scored the job of a lifetime. She's been working for a high-end security company for years, and finally she has a mission all her own: to protect Erin, the Sheikh of Jawhara's wife. But what she thought would be a solo operation suddenly becomes a two-person job. And her partner is none other than Brock Wells, the man who recruited her. The last thing Keira wants is Brock stealing her thunder. But she'll do whatever it takes to succeed.

Brock has been avoiding Kiera since the night he found her fighting some very dangerous men in a bar parking lot. The Slade Security "no fraternization" rule is serious business, and with her mile-long legs, fierce determination, and unwavering focus, Keira is a temptation he can't afford. But with the threat to the sheikha closer than they realized, Brock and Kiera have to go deep undercover, posing as a couple. And suddenly that temptation becomes impossible to ignore…

When their ruse gets a little too real, can Keira and Brock risk letting their guards down? Or will giving in to their feelings put innocent lives in danger?

Grab your copy of *His Stubborn Lover*
www.LeslieNorthBooks.com

BLURB

When Chance McCallister left her to join the Navy SEALS, Mandy Loomis was devastated. Now, more than ten years later, Chance and his brothers are back in town for their father's funeral, but Mandy is no longer that moon-eyed teenager she once was. She's a fiercely independent woman determined to solve her own problems—and she has plenty.

When her gambler father died two years prior, he left Mandy—along with a successful auto repair business—with a ton of debt owed to a ruthless loan shark. Mandy is barely getting by, and when her mechanic quits, she's in a real bind. It just so happens, Chance is willing to help out. Sure, Chance is bigger, stronger, and sexier than ever, but Mandy isn't interested in anything but his mechanical skills. Or maybe just a bit interested in his kissing skills—which, by the way, are just as good as she remembers.

Mandy wasn't the only one brokenhearted when they were just teens. Chance never did get over his first love, and seeing her now only brings back those feelings in a major way. He's grown up a lot since he left their little town, and now that he's home, he's determined to win back the girl he never should have lost. If only he can convince Mandy that he can protect her from the loan shark and his thugs, and that she doesn't have to protect her heart from him.

But just as the two are beginning to realize they're meant to be together, the loan shark makes things more than just a little precarious, putting both their love and their lives in danger.

Grab your copy of *SEAL's Homecoming* (SEAL & Veteran Series Book One) from www.LeslieNorthBooks.com

EXCERPT

Chapter One

Chance McCallister popped the last button and peeled his sweaty Dress White uniform top off with a relieved sigh. For two hours he'd melted under the relentless sun in the long-sleeved polyester. Standing by his father's grave would have been hard enough even without the thick, Georgian, mid-July humidity pressing against the weight of all the medals, ribbons, badges, and Navy SEAL Trident adorning the front of his coat.

"I need a beer." Harris, the middle brother, dropped his Dress Blue uniform top—courtesy of the U.S. Marines—onto the back of a kitchen chair and headed for the refrigerator.

"Grab me one too." Lee, the youngest at twenty-eight, stretched his arms over his head, already losing his Army Dress Blue uniform top the second they got home.

Standing in wet undershirts, uniform pants, belts, and shiny shoes, none of them would pass inspection, but only Harris had to worry about returning to service in thirty days. Chance and Lee each just recently retired from the military, though, for two very different reasons.

"Chance?" Harris held up two bottles by their long necks and arched an eyebrow.

"Yeah," Chance sighed, his skin rippling at the central air conditioning pumping through the vents, drying the moisture. "Might as well."

Harris nudged the door shut with his foot and thrust the bottles at Chance and Lee, then twisted the cap off the one he kept for himself. "To Dad." He lifted his beer. "May he finally be at peace."

Chance tilted his bottle toward his brothers, then took a long, fortifying drink. He'd never expected to become an orphan at thirty years old, but burying his father earlier today had done just that. Ray McCallister had fought a hard battle with liver cancer, but after twenty years of drinking, it had only been a matter of time before the cancer had finally won. Chance had barely been granted retirement from the Navy in time to take care of the bedridden man. Hell, he had only been home a week when Ray died. Harris had always been closest to their father, but Chance used the days he'd been granted before Ray dropped into a coma to make peace. Ray hadn't trusted Chance's attempts at first, assuming they'd fall into old patterns of loud hostile arguments and accusations, but when Chance remained calm and sincere, they'd actually had a few heart-filled conversations. Chance just wished he wasn't so versed in planning funerals. Coordinating his mother's when she died in his teens had left him bereft and filled with resentment. But that was all finally behind him now.

Pivoting, he left the kitchen and wandered into the living room. The small, three-bedroom rancher had seen better days. Worn spots marred the once dark green carpet in the high-traffic paths, and the pale-yellow walls looked tired and faded. Peering out the bay window behind a pillow-style couch, he grunted at how tall the wilting grass had grown on the small plot making up the front yard.

"I mowed last Friday." Chance raised his voice to be heard over his brothers dissecting the attendance at the graveside service. "You two can fight over who's tackling the lawn next."

"Hey, Lee," Harris chirped as he crossed to the fireplace. "Remember this?" Harris plucked an old Polaroid camera from behind Lee's 8x10 high school graduation photo on top of the stained-wood mantel.

Deep creases formed between Lee's brows and he rubbed his right eye. The very eye that had earned him a medical discharge after a small piece of shrapnel had damaged his vision. As a decorated sniper for the Army Rangers, that had been the kiss of death for his career and Lee had refused to start over in another specialization.

"You never went anywhere without that thing." Chance swallowed the last of his beer. "So annoying."

Harris chuckled. "You used to boast about becoming a world-famous photographer."

"Guess the joke's on me," Lee growled, lifting his beer, then chugging the whole thing.

A pang lanced Chance's heart. He needed to figure out a way to reach his brother before this bitter, restless man fully replaced the laughing smartass who loved playing practical jokes.

Setting his bottle onto the closest end table, Chance strolled toward the hallway leading to the bedrooms. "You may have been irritating —" The constant whirring of the photos ejecting out of the bottom used to drive Chance nuts. "—but you did get some great shots." He pointed at a Polaroid picture tucked between the glass and frame of his parents on their wedding day, hanging in the hall.

Harris and Lee crowded on either side of Chance and stared at the photo of their father holding a bag of boiled peanuts, caught mid-shock when he walked into the house for his surprise birthday party.

"Oh, man." Harris cracked up. "Look at his face. I forgot about that day."

"But this one's my favorite." Chance plucked a Polaroid out of another frame. The entire family—three brothers and both parents—stood in front of the house on a sunny day only months before their mother got sick. "I still can't believe you talked Mrs. Mabry into taking it." Their old neighbor, seventy-one at the time, had always complained about everything and everyone.

Lee smirked and for a moment, his amber-brown eyes twinkled like they used to. "That old bird was easy to figure out. The second I promised to scoop all the poop out of her yard and dump it on Pete Walsh's porch, she was putty in my hands."

A bark of laughter erupted from Chance's throat. That damn dog had been a menace and Pete had only cared about collecting disability checks. Replacing the photo, he peered up the hall, then back toward the living room. "Can either of you picture living here anymore?"

Tension leached the small bit of levity.

Their father had worked two jobs in an effort to keep a roof over their heads and their mother's medical bills from consuming him. He hadn't been able to save anything extra to pass down, so he'd only left the three of them the house as their inheritance.

"I think we should sell it," Lee announced, turning away and tromping down the hall.

"You don't want to stay now that you're out?" Chance asked, following behind.

Lee paused in the living room. "Are you saying *you* want to stay?" His amber eyes shuttered. "You're out too. You think Springwell is going to welcome you with open arms?"

The muscle in Chance's jaw ticked. For most of his teenage years, their hometown of Springwell, Georgia, had not been the kindest to him. Living in a small town meant no transgression was ever truly forgiven or forgotten. And no matter how unfair, Chance had a reputation as a fighter. It didn't matter that he never started the fights, his tendency to do whatever it took to protect a weaker person from being hurt or bullied meant he settled a lot of situations with his fists. It didn't take a genius to figure out all the suppressed anger at his mother's death, and the constant butting heads with his dad had just added to his willingness to pound on someone else.

Thankfully, twelve years in the Navy—with eight of them as a SEAL —had given him an outlet for the rage until he no longer had to channel it. The type of bond he had formed with his teammates had given him the emotional support he hadn't realized he needed until his confidence grew with each successful mission and the vise squeezing his chest disappeared.

"You're probably right. This town's going to have the same opinion of me as before." Chance drove his fingers through his messy hair still slick with sweat. "I can't say I want to stay, but I didn't exactly have enough time to figure out what comes next when I retired. Dad's health nosedived even before I landed on this doorstep, and I've been focused on that ever since." He eyed his brothers. "Harris only has bereavement leave, but what about you, Lee? What are you going to do now?"

Lee sneered. "I doubt Springwell has a need for a useless sniper in SWAT—not that we're big enough to even have a dedicated unit." He swished his hand over his high-and-tight shorn head. "Nothing's holding me here, but I have no clue where to go."

"You're not useless," Harris snapped, rounding on Lee. "You've still got the skills no matter what the Army says."

"Agreed." Chance jabbed a finger at the youngest brother. Lee's unit had dubbed him "Puma" after his eye color and the way the large cat was also a solitary killer, hunting its prey just like a sniper, stalking its target with patience and strategy. "Your vision may not meet Ranger qualifications anymore, but I'd bet my life if I slapped a rifle in your hands, you'd nail the center of a bull's eye with ease."

Lee's chin jutted mulishly, but he didn't say a word. Instead, he sauntered into the kitchen and opened the door into the single-car garage. "How's this coming?"

Getting the message to back off, Chance stepped into the sweltering garage and his muscles loosened at the sight before him. A black 1967 Ford Shelby Mustang sat with its hood propped up, facing the garage door. His father had found the classic muscle car in an auction years ago, but had never gotten it running. The body was in pristine condition but whoever owned it before didn't know jack about engines. To be fair, their dad hadn't had much of a clue either. In their family, Chance was the only one who really knew what he was doing under a hood.

"I think I might be close to getting it started." Chance fingered the blanket he had spread along the fender to keep it from getting dinged by tools or parts. Working on the car had given him a modicum of peace the past week. A much-needed outlet after watching his father die, then all the fallout of dealing with notifying banks, companies, insurance, etcetera while planning the funeral. "In fact, the carburetor I ordered should be in today at the shop." He picked up a wrench off the multi-colored quilt. "I took a risk and ordered a much cheaper one that's supposed to be equivalent to the original Holley. Not ideal, but I wanted to keep my savings instead of blowing it on original parts."

"The shop, huh?" Harris asked, his voice sing-songy.

Chance stiffened.

Grab your copy of *SEAL's Homecoming* (SEAL & Veteran Series Book One) from www.LeslieNorthBooks.com

www.ingramcontent.com/pod-product-compliance
Lightning Source LLC
Chambersburg PA
CBHW071942150726
47999CB00001B/291